(The T

MW00882521

By Nikki Wild

Copyright 2016 Nikki Wild

All Rights Reserved

Find me at my website:

WWW.WILDNIKKI.COM

Or friend me on Facebook!

http://www.facebook.com/wildnikki

Prologue

"I'm not going," I protested, firmly shaking my head. My black Frey boot tapped against the trendy cement floor of the restaurant.

My mother and her boss sat across the table from me. Bear Dalton, Chairman and CEO of Dalton Enterprises, crossed his sculpted arms over his chest, his deep blue eyes peering at me, his expression serious and somber.

You can't intimidate me, I thought to myself, meeting his piercing gaze. He wasn't *my* boss. He was my mother's boss. I'd only met him once before and I didn't know he was going to be here today.

"Look, Mom, you can go without me," I said, turning back to my mother as I tried to muster a smile. Mom had worked her ass off for this job. She was one of *those* women. You know the type. Relentlessly ambitious, never satisfied with breaking just one glass ceiling, she wanted to break through them all.

She was on a mission to do just that. She'd been working for Bear's firm for the last ten years, quickly working her way up the ladder, constantly vying for promotion after promotion.

And here it was — her golden ticket.

This job that Bear had offered her — Chief Financial Officer of Dalton

Enterprises - was her latest obsession. I don't use that word lightly. When Mom committed to something, she went all in. It went way past the point of commitment.

Trust me, I should know.

Our relationship has been the lone casualty of her undying devotion to her career. She missed so many school events that by the time I'd graduated from high school, most of my classmates were convinced I didn't have parents at all.

It might as well have been that way.

My father left us high and dry years ago, his fantasy of greener pastures being fulfilled in the arms of a twenty-one year old intern in sunny Sausalito when I was just a baby.

Growing up, it was just the two of us, but Mom was rarely there, so really, it was mostly just me. That's why I couldn't believe she was being so insistent on me moving to New York with her. Let her go to New York on her own.

What the hell did she need me for?

"You know I won't be able to focus with you so far away, Chloe," she insisted, her perfectly coiffed blonde bob bouncing around her face. "You can't do this to me!"

Of course, it wasn't that she cared about me, it was all about her.

It was always about her.

Despite never being around, she still wouldn't let me be independent. She had some screwed up Mother Theresa complex. It was almost like the fact that I didn't need her made her want me to need her even more. And yet she was never there in the first place. It was all screwed up and twisted.

I shouldn't be making a scene in front of her boss, I knew that, but it was her fault because she'd cornered me like this. She'd invited me to lunch, teasing me with some 'exciting news' to share. I should have known something was up when she told me to meet her at Departure, the trendy sushi joint on top of the Nine's hotel in downtown Portland.

It wasn't that she didn't do swanky, it's just that she usually reserved going to places like that for business meetings or to impress clients.

Or her boss.

I knew he'd be here even before I saw the handsome man sitting at the table with her. I wasn't expecting her to tell me she was moving to New York, and I sure as hell wasn't expecting her to insist that I join her.

"My life is here. My friends. My apartment. I'm out of school and I'm looking for a job. I'll be fine without you. You'll be fine without me…"

"This isn't up for negotiation, Chloe," she exclaimed, her voice a sharp knife of motherly disapproval, even though the smile on her face desperately tried to hide her anger. "Bear has given me an extraordinary opportunity, darling. New York is an exciting city. We've never lived there before. You'll love it."

I took a deep breath and stood up from the table.

"I'm twenty-six years old. I'm a grown-ass woman. We'll be just fine living in separate cities. It's time you let me go," I said.

"But New York —," she insisted.

"—New York is full of rats! It's overcrowded, cold, and it smells like a sewer!" I interrupted. "Give it up. The answer is no!" I squared my shoulders, grabbed my purse and turned away, mustering all my strength as I put one foot in front of the other and walked out to the huge balcony looking out over the city.

"I'll talk to her," a deep voice boomed from behind. I ignored him and kept walking as I looked down on the Christmas lights and glittering Christmas tree standing in the center of Pioneer Square below. Mom hated when I walked away from her, but she was already mad at me, so I figured why not go all out and stir the pot a little more.

She was never going to forgive me now anyway.

I wasn't about to leave this city. *My city.* I loved living in Portland.

All the grey, dreary days, the endless misty rain from October through June, finally falling away into long, blissful days of warm, lush summers. Our summers are short, but something about putting up with all the darkness seems to make it that much brighter once it finally does arrive. The landscape burst with flowers of every type, starting with the cherry blossoms in the spring and followed by the sweet scent of roses trailing down every street all summer long.

It's a stunning city.

Sure, right now, it's smack dab in the middle of the dreary season, but spring would finally arrive eventually. I wasn't about to miss it.

New York, on the other hand, I could do without.

I'd been there once on a quick trip with a bunch of girlfriends during my Freshman year in college. I was so excited—sure it was going to be the trip of a lifetime. I couldn't wait to spend my days shopping in funky vintage stores, exploring the warehouses of the garment district in Manhattan and spend my nights going to Broadway shows and world famous nightclubs.

We'd done all of that, but it had been incredibly exhausting. There was so much walking. Just one block was the size of three Portland blocks and everything was at least a hundred blocks apart. And forget taking taxi's everywhere — they were way too expensive.

We were forced to walk past the wildest sidewalk scenes, which were peppered with the constant appearance of rats the size of large cats and the incessant smell of urine that stayed in my hair for weeks after I'd returned home.

I hated every second of it.

The Big Apple might be the center of the fashion industry but as far as I was concerned, I wasn't in any hurry to get there. I was content to stay right here in Portland and open a small, boutique shop of my own, without a rat in sight. Besides, Portland was quickly becoming a hub of up and coming fashion designers. I was determined to be one of them.

The winter breeze and light drizzle had me shivering. I'd left my sweater at the table, leaving my shoulders bare. I flinched when I felt a hot hand touch my shoulder.

I turned and came face to face with Bear Dalton.

"Hello, Chloe," he said, his voice a deep velvety growl.

"Hello, Mr. Dalton," I replied.

"Let's talk," he said, squeezing my bare shoulder. The warmth of his hand was searing my skin, his touch so intimate that it shook me to my very core.

"Excuse me?" I asked, shrugging my shoulder away from his hand.

His eyes peered into mine, the darkest, deepest, bluest gaze.

"Just a quick word, Chloe. Come with me, please," he said, walking back inside and throwing a stern look over his shoulder. I hesitated for a quick second, but my feet began moving on their own and then there I was—walking behind him slowly, drinking in his fit frame, his perfectly tailored black suit, his expensive Italian loafers, and cursing the manners that had been beaten into my brain at the same time.

Later, I would think back to this moment, wondering if that's where it all went wrong. What would have happened if I hadn't followed him? If I'd decided being polite to Mom's boss wasn't my responsibility?

But I did.

Willingly.

With only a moment's hesitation, I followed him like a loyal labrador follows his master.

The dimly lit hallways of the restaurant wound through the place like a maze. Whispered conversations from the patrons at the low slung tables floated through the air as we walked past. I turned my head, catching a glimpse of myself in a gilded mirror hanging on the wall, but my eyes quickly darted back to Bear.

The deep blue lighting made his wavy black hair shimmer like jewels. He turned down another hallway and then opened an unmarked door, waving me in before him.

I looked inside—a private dining room, with white suede couches lining the mirrored walls. My stomach fluttered as I looked back at Bear, the demanding look in his eye catching me off guard.

"I don't think —," I began, shaking my head.

"Go on in," he said, gently placing his hand on my elbow and guiding me inside.

"Mr. Dalton, I —," I protested as I walked in, turning back to watch as he closed and locked the door behind him. He turned to me, a slow smile spreading across his face. I took a deep breath and tried to relax.

"Chloe, I've told you already—call me Bear, okay?" My heart was pounding and I nodded. "Bear, right. Listen, my mother will be just fine without me. There's really no need for you to waste your time trying to persuade me to move. She's just—"

"— No, Chloe. Listen to me," he interrupted, his voice a low husky growl as he closed the distance between us. He brought his face close to mine, so close I could smell his musky cologne. "Your mother cares about you. She cares about this job and she's unbelievably good at it. I want her for the position, and I'm not afraid to *take* what I want. Do you understand?"

"Yes," I nodded, my heart racing. The darkness of his eyes was mesmerizing, and now that they were this close, I couldn't help but remember the last time I'd seen the tiny golden flecks scattered throughout the deepest blue I'd ever seen. I'd only met Bear once before, at a company Christmas party a few years ago. He'd unnerved me then and he was doing it again.

"But I don't need to be there—," I continued my protest.

"—No. You're coming to New York, Chloe," he said, firmly.

"I'm not," I said, finally finding my voice, even though it was shaking. I lifted my chin defiantly and cringed when he laughed softly.

"You've always intrigued me, Chloe," he said, those ocean eyes squinting at me, his full lips turning up at the corners again. "You're strong, aren't you? Determined. Won't take no for an answer. I like that," he reached up, pushing a strand of hair behind my ear, bringing his face even closer as lowered his voice. "We have that in common."

I was speechless. Bear Dalton knew nothing about me. We'd shared one dance at that company Christmas party my mother had dragged me to and I hadn't seen him since.

Here he was, thinking he knew me inside and out. Who did he think he was?

"Unfortunately for you," he continued. "I never lose."

"Is that so?" I asked, hating the quivering in my voice.

He was so arrogant! Sure, he was fucking handsome. And he's probably richer than the King of England.

And yeah, okay, he's got that fucking body - the one that could melt most women into puddles of sex, but so what?

He wasn't really my type.

He was ten years older than me, first of all.

Did he really think lowering his voice and flashing those smoldering eyes at me would get me to change my mind? What kind of weak, naive woman did he think I was?

"Would you like a demonstration?" he asked, cocking his head to the side, a teasing smile lifting the corners of his full lips even wider. My breath caught in my throat.

"A what?" I asked, my eyes widening as I watched his hand reach up again, his fingertip tracing my jaw and down to my chin, then trailing down to my neck. I swallowed hard as his fingers wrapped around my narrow neck and ever-so-gently squeezed for a fraction of a second, before sliding around to the back of my neck.

I shivered at his touch, his boldness shocking me.

His fingers snaked into my hair slowly. And then, ever so slightly, he squeezed, pulling my head back as he pulled down.

I gasped, my eyes wide with disbelief, my mouth wide open in surprise. Before I could say a word to protest, his mouth crashed onto mine.

I froze. Waves of pain shot through my head, his fingers tightening their grip as his tongue dove into my mouth, tangling with my own.

He towered over me, kissing me deeply as I whimpered, my body softening below him. When I felt his arm slide around my waist and his body press against mine, the rock-hard erection pressing into my belly, a low moan escaped from me.

He tore his mouth away and his eyes clashed with mine. A slow, satisfied smile spread across his face and he nodded slowly.

"That's what I thought," he murmured, before smashing his lips into mine again. His kiss was deep, exploring, so hot, his tongue skillfully pulling every ounce of pleasure from my body. He pulled his fingers from my hair and brought his hands to my shoulders, gently pushing me back until I was up against the table, his body pressing into mine, his cock hard and throbbing and so hot I could feel the heat through our clothes.

Before I knew what was happening, my hand flew up, slapping his incredibly handsome face as hard as I possibly could.

I was so confused. What the fuck had just happened?

His eyes flashed with amusement as he touched his cheek, and a slow smile spread across his face.

"Did that feel good?" he asked.

"No!" I replied, my voice shaking. It didn't feel good. Not at all.

"Then don't do it again," he said, his low growl a stern warning.

"Bear, I —," I began, shaking my head in confusion, my lips on fire from his kiss.

His hands interrupted me. They were everywhere all at once. Sliding over the curve of my breasts, trailing down my belly and over my hips, until he was lifting up the edge of my skirt and I was letting him, watching with wide eyes as the fabric slid up over my hips.

In a flash, he ripped my red lace panties from my body as easily as if they were made of tissue, throwing them on the ground at our feet.

"What are you doing!" I cried, my eyes wide, my brain reeling in shock.

"You wore those for me, didn't you?" he asked.

I whimpered when I felt the air on my naked pussy. His lush lips landed back on mine, kissing me as my protests died away in his mouth and turned to soft moans.

His tongue searched mine while his fingers found my center, plunging inside smoothly. My thighs fell open, welcoming his touch as waves of pleasure shot through my body, his fingers expertly pressing upwards, leaving me weak in the knees, my entire body shaking in shocked pleasure.

Quickly, he pulled his hand out of my pussy and tore his lips from mine.

"Open," he whispered, sliding a finger in my mouth, the taste of my own pussy filling my mouth as my tongue twirled around his finger. I met his gaze, my questioning eyes daringly meeting his, a hint of mischievousness sparkling brightly in them before he turned me around quickly and bent me over the table.

A quick rustle of clothing, the sound of a falling zipper and in an instant — hardness.

Throbbing, thick, hot—his cock pressed against my willing depths. I strained and cried out as he sheathed his thickness deep inside me, biting my lip in a vain attempt to keep myself quiet even as I was stretched beyond anything I'd ever thought possible. I braced myself, my breasts smashed hard against the wooden table as he drew himself out and in, pleasure rolling through my body with his rhythmic movement. His cock was deliciously hot, piercing my sex with expert precision, his strokes full and hard and purposeful.

It was unbelievable. My entire being was submitting to the exquisite and unexpected assault.

I arched my back, forgetting where I was, who I was with—*who I was.* I lifted my ass higher for him, opening myself up to his thundering thrusts. His cock was massive, rocking into me from behind, sending shivers of unending pleasure shooting through my body.

My breasts heaved as I gasped for air, his powerful thrusts leaving me breathless and shaking as he continued to drive deep into me with relentless force. He reached up, grabbing a handful of hair again and pulling my head back to him.

I turned my head, opening my mouth, his hot tongue sliding inside of me as he fucked into me over and over.

"Now, darling Chloe, listen to me, okay?" he growled as he tore his lips away again, his fingers firmly tangled in my long black hair, his mouth brushing hotly against my ear. I nodded, my body on fire for him as he continued.

"You're going to be a good girl. A very, very, good girl. You're going to come to New York. You're going to do everything I say. And you're going to work for *me*, do you understand?"

Confusion flashed in my eyes, my mouth opening in shock.

His cock throbbed and swelled inside of me and he fucked into me harder and harder, thrusting in with each word, slowing pulling out and slamming me harder against the table as he pushed back into my dripping center.

"Tell me you agree, Beauty," he demanded, pulling my hair a little harder. "Tell me you'll come to New York before I cum in your tight little pussy."

My mind reeled but all I could focus on was how deliciously huge and hard he was, how I had never felt such intense pleasure shooting through my body like this before and how I thought I would surely shrivel up and die if he stopped now.

I needed this more than I'd ever needed anything. Him, his cock, his body pounding into mine.

I would have done anything for him at that point, just so that he never stopped.

But New York? *A job? What kind of job?*

As if he sensed my hesitation, he pulled his cock free from my body.

"Don't stop," I begged, wiggling my ass, pressing back towards him. "Please, Bear, don't stop."

"Tell me what I want to hear," he growled, his tongue darting out and sliding along my ear, the rumbling vibration of his voice going right to my throbbing clit. "If you can't obey me, then this is over before it begins. Your poor mother would be so disappointed…" He pushed his hardness inside me again, driving delicious deep then pulling out completely once more. His hands were resting on my hips, the head of his cock resting on my ass.

I whimpered at his absence, my head shaking in protest.

"No, no," I begged, pressing back towards him.

I didn't know what the hell he was offering me. All I knew was that I didn't want him to stop. I needed him to finish what he started. I needed his cock slamming into me harder and harder until I came. I was starving for him, and as he pulled my hair again, pulling my head back until I met his gaze, I knew what I had to do.

"What's the answer, Beauty?" he said, the slow smile returning to his gorgeous face as he reached down and slid his cock along the lips of my wet pussy. "In, or out?"

My pussy spasmed, unsatisfied, yearning for his hardness. Suddenly, I realized I didn't care about anything else. Nothing else mattered. I knew I'd do anything this man wanted as long as he didn't stop fucking me.

I nodded, tears stinging my eyes as I pushed back into him.

"In," I said. "I'll go to New York."

"And?" he asked, teasing me, rubbing the head of his perfect cock against my entrance. "Will you be a *good* girl?"

"I'll be good," I gasped, lifting my ass like a wanton hussy, pushing back towards him. I didn't care, though. I only had one care in the world right now and it was him. I needed his cock now that I'd had it and I knew I'd never stop.

"What else?" he growled.

"I'll do anything," I whispered, my heart racing in my chest.

"Ah, that's it," he said, rubbing the head of his cock against my entrance teasingly.

"Please, Bear!" I begged. "Please!"

He slid back inside of me, the soft skin of his cock like velvet against my own softness.

He fucked me—deeply, roughly, skillfully—until I was shaking and writhing on the end of his hardness, our bodies exploding together in an Earth shattering burst of sensation that destroyed everything I'd ever believed about myself, a volcano of emotion that changed the very core of my identity, leaving nothing remaining in its wake but a clean slate, rendering me starving for knowledge about myself that only Bear would prove to possess.

* * *

His hand was hot against the small of my back as he led me back to the table.

Mom was waiting and looked up from her phone with a smile.

"You're back!" she said. "I was beginning to think you both left me here."

"Sorry about that," Bear said, pulling back my chair like a perfect gentleman. "We were talking, but I think we made some progress. Didn't we, Chloe?"

"Yes," I replied, swallowing hard, trying desperately to hide what had just happened. My face flushed and covered in small beads of sweat as I closed my thighs together tightly.

"I'll go to New York with you, Mom."

"What! You will? That's wonderful," Mom's eyes lit up with joy."

"It'll be okay, I think," I said quietly, embarrassment running through me like lightning as bear caught me with his gaze. "I have to go... I'm meeting some friends later."

"Oh," she replied. "Okay, well, call me tomorrow." She leaned up and gave me a light touch on the shoulder. "Thank you. You have no idea what this means to me."

"I understand," I said. I nodded at Bear silently, my body shivering with pleasure as he flashed a nonchalant smile. I grabbed my sweater and my purse and turned and walked away, my legs quivering with every step.

"What did you do to convince her?" I heard Mom ask Bear as I walked away.

"I offered her a job," he replied lightly.

His words would linger in my ears all night, but his touch buzzed against my skin for days.

Chapter 1

Sometimes, you see the fork. Sometimes, you don't.

Sometimes, your life takes a turn and you don't really have a choice.

Every now and then, changes come hurling at you and you don't even see them coming.

And then, there they are—unavoidable, in your face, ugly, messy—demanding you acknowledge them.

Or, maybe they aren't so harsh at first. But that's how they get you, you know?

They're sly and charming, pulling you in with a smile and maybe a promise of something sweet and then, before you know it, there you are—falling to your knees to do whatever it takes to get another taste of paradise.

But I'm getting ahead of myself. I haven't fallen to my knees just yet, but we'll get there, don't worry.

What I'm trying to tell you is that I didn't see it coming at first. I didn't see any of it coming. How could I? I was naive, really.

Sure, I'm a grown-ass woman, but even at twenty-six there are days when I still feel eighteen.

To say that I had led a sheltered and bland existence before that day at the restaurant with Bear would be the understatement of the year.

I'd managed to graduate college without much in the way of experience… I'd had one boyfriend throughout college—the infamous Harlan Lewis, as my friends called him. Our relationship was full of drama. *A lot of drama.*

He was charming and cocky, at first. He drew me out of my shell by showering me with attention and affection. I'd never had a boyfriend that was so doting before, but he had a few shortcomings. Sex was all about him, and it was over in an instant. I had no time to be excited, much less satisfied.

In the beginning, I told myself that sex didn't matter. Things would get better.

But they didn't. They only got worse.

After a year of dating, his attention turned to suffocating possessiveness. Then he accused me of cheating on him.

One night, he slapped me after I came home late from happy hour with my friends.

That's all it took.

I mean, I should have left a lot sooner, I know, but I wasn't about to hang around and be someone's punching bag.

I got over him quicker than it takes for a good Oregon shower to run through town. Six months later, he still texts me trying to get back together.

As if I'd sink so low ever again.

I wanted a lot more from a partner than Harlan could ever provide.

I was ready for all the breathless orgasms I was supposed to be having at my age.

I'd certainly read all about them. In fact, I'd spent hours upon hours haunting the romance section at Powell's bookstore, walking out with bags full of deliciously trashy novels, hoping nobody on the Max peeked in my bags on the way home.

I couldn't wait to see what it felt like for my breasts to heave or my stomach to flutter with desire as my lover gazed at me through hooded lids.

I wanted all of that stuff. I'd never even come close to feeling like that with Harlan. I was starting to think I'd never feel it…

I mean, I didn't see those things in my near future—but I was ready and waiting, just in case.

There were a few things in the way, of course.

My shyness, for one. I wasn't a flirt, not like my friend Marie. She didn't hold back, not for a second. When she saw someone she was interested in, she went at them with both guns blazing.

Me? I just turned and ran the other way. The few times I'd gone out on dates in college (outside of what Marie and I now called my 'Harlan period') had ended in excruciating awkwardness. When the date was over I'd lay there for hours, staring up at the cracked ceiling of my apartment, wondering—*is this it? Is this really all there is?*

Sex wasn't fun. It wasn't exciting. There were no hooded lids, no heaving breasts anywhere to be found. I would have given anything to even feel a little quiver in my stomach, but nope—no flutters, no butterflies.

I guess you could say I gave up after I broke up with Harlan. Trying to find someone else seemed like so much work. I stopped thinking it would ever happen and I turned myself off to the possibility of ever meeting someone who made my toes curl.

I had my bad boy book boyfriends and that was enough.

I dove into my semester at school, learning everything I could about fashion design and focused all my energy on creating my own line of dresses. School and work became my life.

That's why I was blindsided today. Sure, maybe I'd put those little red panties on because I had some misguided little fantasy in my head, but I never expected a man like Bear to make that fantasy real… I never expected him to make me feel like that.

There he was—bigger than life, utterly intimidating, his demanding presence so grand and hulking that I was left breathless just by staring up at him. I mean, I felt a quiver in my stomach as soon as he'd closed that door behind us—and that had to mean something, right?

I just didn't know what.

I didn't know that this was my fork.

Bear Dalton. Chairman and CEO of Dalton Enterprises, the premier development firm in America, my Mother's billionaire boss. He was the man who made my toes curl, my breasts heave, and my pussy sing.

How could I have ever said no to that?

Chapter 2

Relentless throbbing pain shot through my brain as the phone next to my head buzzed. I rolled over and looked at the clock, a loud groan escaping from my mouth. It wasn't even seven yet. I didn't need to look at my cell to see who was calling, I knew it was my Mother.

'Early bird catches the worm, Chloe,'— I could still hear her high-pitched mantra singing in my head, even after all these years. She'd woken me up every morning as a child with that stupid saying and it was forever etched onto my brain.

There were times where I was certain I was adopted or switched at birth. Considering she'd raised me alone, you'd think that would have bonded us more, that maybe I'd have adopted some her characteristics over time, but we couldn't have been more different or more distant.

Not only was she an early riser compared to me being content to sleep way past noon, but she was so fucking ambitious. She never stopped. She never took a day off. She never took her eye off of the proverbial prize.

I was more of a 'be here now' kind of girl. I stopped and smelled every rose in my path, savored every morsel of life that I could. I could sit for hours, letting the day float away and just people watch.

Not my Mother. She was constantly moving, insisting time was money all along the way. It was exhausting. *She* was exhausting.

And the fact that she was attempting to wake me up way before seven in the morning on a fucking Saturday was exhausting. I threw the phone across my bedroom and shoved a pillow over my head.

I'd call her later. After I'd had time to think.

I'd been so blown away by my experience with Bear last night that I'd come straight home, cancelled my plans with my friends, and sat on my couch getting up close and personal to a cheap red wine. I did my best to make some sense out of what had happened.

It didn't work.

I was still just as confused as I had been when I'd left. I was also very sore—in the most absolutely delicious way.

My body was still on fire with Bear's touch and now that I was awake again, thanks to my Mother, I couldn't ignore the fact that all I wanted was to feel him inside of me again.

"So much for sleeping," I groaned, throwing the covers off my naked body. I'd fallen asleep with my hands tucked between my legs, desperately trying to quench the fire that Bear had ignited within my body, and now there they were again—furiously rubbing at my clit, hoping to find some magical illusive release that would give me a break from thinking about him, yearning for him, if only for a few minutes.

Dizzy and fuzzy, my brain began replaying the scene from yesterday like a movie in my head. I could still hear his voice, see those deep blue eyes peering into mine as if he was pouring himself into my soul.

I barely knew this man but somehow he'd managed to crawl inside of me and take up residence, in a spot so deep and dark that I never even knew it was there. In the depths of my intoxication last night, I'd imagined Bear doing things to me that I'd never thought of before. I'd gone places I'd never taken myself, holding his hand the entire way.

What had happened to me?

Look, I wasn't one of those naive girls that really believes some magical man is going to show up with some magical, rainbow-shooting cock that is going to transport to me to some everlasting heaven.

I know those books I read aren't real. They're *fantasies*. An escape from the ho-hum days of boring routines we're all forced to play out just to survive and put food on the table.

As much as I wanted them to come true, I didn't really expect Mr. Toe Curler and all my fantasies to actually materialize.

I was a reasonable girl. Hell, part of me didn't really even believe that stuff existed at all, especially after enduring all of Harlan's bullshit. I'd put up with so much shit from him and gotten nothing in return.

Not one heart-racing moment.

Not one breathless kiss.

Certainly not an orgasm.

It wouldn't have taken much to make me happy right now. I would have been satisfied with a short-lived butterfly or two in my stomach from a first kiss.

That's why I never, in a million, gazillion years, thought something like this would be real. That a man like Bear Dalton would be real. That a man like Bear Dalton would want a woman like *me.*

There were times when Harlan's possessive nature might have been a turn on, but he did everything wrong. His every move was selfish.

With Bear, something was different.

Very different.

Bear made me quiver with every word he'd uttered. His demanding orders had only made my body shiver with exquisite anticipation. He left me wanting more in the most perfect way possible—because it had been so delectably wrong and so precisely satisfying. It was like someone handed him a map to my body. Once he'd started fucking me, it was obvious he knew exactly how to please me.

He'd found the spot.

That spot in my brain that had been begging for someone to turn it on. The spot that was desperate for the kind of attention a man like this could demand.

I don't know how he found it.

I don't know why it was *him*, of all people.

I don't have any idea what the future holds, but I do know one thing—I wouldn't turn this opportunity down if my life depended on it.

And maybe it does.

Maybe this will turn out to be the worst thing I've ever agreed to in my life. Maybe it'll even be worse than Harlan. Maybe I'll go running back to Portland with my tail between my legs.

But maybe I won't. Maybe it's exactly what I've needed all this time.

My hands worked faster and faster, my fingers sliding inside of my pussy faster as I imagined it was Bear's throbbing cock inside of me. I felt the first waves of my orgasm crash as Bear's face was front and center in my imagination. Those teasing, demanding eyes beckoned me as I submitted to his memory one more beautiful time.

* * *

"Hey Mom," I finally answered one of her *many* phone calls two hours later. I'd dragged myself out of bed, showered and eaten and was finally feeling strong enough to face a conversation with my her.

"Chloe, please tell me you aren't just waking up," she said.

I rolled my eyes and ignored her question completely. She didn't really want to know or care, she only wanted to judge me. I could do that just fine on my own.

"What's up, Mom?" I asked.

"What job did Dalton offer you?" she asked, getting right to the point. She was never one for small talk or beating around the bush.

"Didn't you ask him that?" I asked. I had no idea what job I would be doing. So far, the only work I've done wasn't anything she wanted to hear about. If Bear had other ideas, he hadn't communicated them to me.

"He was vague," she said. I could almost see her eyebrows wrinkle disapprovingly through the phone.

"He was vague with me, too," I said.

"How much is he paying you?" she asked.

"I don't know, Mom," I replied, growing frustrated with her inquisition.

"Then why would you accept?" she demanded.

I sighed, knowing there was no way in hell I could tell her the truth. Part of me hadn't figured out the answer to that just yet. All I knew was that I'd never felt more alive than those few moments alone with Bear and I couldn't help but chase that feeling.

"I love you, Mom," I said. "I just want you to be happy."

"Bullshit," she said. "He really didn't mention a salary? Benefits?"

"I'm sure it'll be plenty of money. Besides, isn't this what you've always wanted?"

"But what about your career?" she asked. My breath caught in my throat for a second. Was she really thinking about what was good for me? "You just graduated with an art degree. That's hardly going to transfer to working for a development company. I don't know what Bear was thinking…"

I wondered the same thing. *What was he thinking? Was he thinking about me? Was he at home somewhere thinking about me right now? Was he laughing about the naive woman he manipulated?*

"Mom, I'll figure it out. It doesn't matter about the job. If I don't like it, I'll find something else once we get settled. I'm doing this for *you*. Besides, you've been trying to get me to take an entry position with the company for years."

"Yes, but Bear Dalton can be a demanding boss," she said in a tone of warning.

"Maybe that's exactly what I need right now."

"Hmmm," she murmured. "I guess that's always a possibility. Chloe, I really think you'll find that New York has a lot of opportunities for a woman like you."

"I know, Mom," I replied. "I learned from the best."

"That's sweet," she said. "Okay, I'll get everything arranged. The movers will be coming to your place to pack up and ship all your things on Monday…"

She launched into business mode, her rare show of warmth replaced by her short, clipped barrage of instructions.

No wonder Bear wants her to be his CFO, I thought to myself.

Chapter 3

"I can't believe you're leaving me," Marie said, as she folded up my favorite sweater, her fuzzy curly red hair sprouting wildly from her head. She'd shown up a few minutes ago to help me pack. We'd ordered pizza and opened a bottle of wine and gotten to work. "And so quickly! I don't even have time to throw you a party!"

"I know," I replied. "I'm sorry that it's all so sudden."

"I just don't understand how she convinced you," she said. "I would have thought you'd have used this opportunity to put some distance between you and Matilda, once and for all."

Marie and I had been friends since middle school. We'd met in a painting class at daVinci Arts Middle School—the school that parents sent their weird artsy kids to that they didn't know what else to do with.

We were the most timid of our whole class when we'd first arrived, in awe of the bigger, cooler, artsy kids on the verge of high school, most of them already sporting dyed hair and Doc Martens. Marie blossomed, quickly adapting to the quirky unstructured atmosphere. She surrounding herself with all the cool kids.

I was like a fish out of water.

My classmates were performers—loud, wild, constantly moving and expressing themselves. I'd spent my childhood cutting out paper dolls and then making my own clothes for them, eventually moving to sewing real ones, but I'd spent most of my time tucked away in a corner all by myself.

Marie quickly recognized that I was struggling. She took me under her wing, made sure to include me in everything and dared anyone to say a cross word about me, even though my shyness was painful at times.

After a while, she managed to make me feel comfortable and in my own way, I guess I blossomed too. We've been inseparable ever since. We endured high school and college together and we always thought we'd still be standing next to each other after graduation.

I couldn't blame her for being upset about this. I'd upended our entire plan.

"I don't know why I agreed," I said, feeling awful for lying to her. "I just wanted to make her happy, I guess."

"Making your mother happy is not usually a priority for you," she said, eyeing me suspiciously. "Are you sure there isn't something you aren't telling me?"

"Well," I hesitated. Marie knew me better than anyone. Of course she would sniff this out. "I sort of…connected…with my Mom's boss."

"What do you mean, connected?" she asked, squinting her eyes.

"Honestly," I replied, relieved to let the words spill out of me. "Marie, if you tell anyone about this I'll die… It was unexpected! He just came in and took charge…I didn't really know what to do. And then it was so fucking incredible…" I was breathless just thinking about Bear's hands on me.

"What the hell are you talking about? Slow down. Start from the beginning," she said, sitting on my bed.

"Okay," I said, sinking into the comfort of the quilt my Grandma had sewn for me. "I wasn't going to go. I told my mother I wasn't interested in moving to New York. God, do you remember how big those fucking rats were? But then Bear sort of…changed my mind."

"Bear?" she asked, cocking her head to the side.

"Yeah. His name is Bear Dalton."

"Your Mom's boss's name is Bear? For fuck's sake! Who names their kid Bear? Why didn't you ever tell me this?"

"I don't know. But he's certainly not a kid," I said, a slow smile spreading across my face. I could still feel him inside me, my skin was still burning from his touch, even days later. "And I guess he's my boss now, too."

"He gave you a job? Why didn't you say so?"

"I'm telling you now!"

"Well, what is it? How much does it pay?"

"You sound like Matilda! I - I - don't really know…" I murmured, my voice trailing off as I realized how ridiculous this all sounded now that I was putting it into words.

"What do you mean you don't know?" she laughed.

"Alright, look. He fucked me."

"What!" Her mouth practically fell on the floor.

"I mean, we had sex…" A blush crept up my face. Marie and I talked about sex all the time but for some reason I felt like this was different. Should I have been ashamed about what happened? Should I have kept it to myself? There's no way in hell I could have kept this from Marie much longer.

"You had sex with your Mom's boss? That's kind of…hot," she smiled.

"My boss, too, technically," I shrugged.

"So let me get this straight," she laughed. "You fucked your new boss but you don't know how much he's going to pay you or what the job is but you've agreed to move clear across the country to do this mystery job?"

"Basically, yes," I said.

"Damn. That's insane. He must have been one incredible lay," she shook her head.

"There wasn't any lying down involved, he bent me over the table in a private room at Departure," I said.

Her laughter roared through my apartment.

"Sounds romantic," she managed to spit out through her hysterical laughter.

I shook my head, second guessing my decision to confide in her.

"Look, it's crazy, believe me I know that. He just…damn, he just had this pull. He's so fucking handsome. And sophisticated. And rich. And sexy as hell…"

"Oh, my god! I have to see this guy," she said, grabbing my computer and punching in Bear's name on a google search page. Hundreds of pictures popped up, just as I knew they would, because I'd already spent hours and hours searching for info on Bear myself last night.

"Holy fuck," Marie whispered. "He doesn't even look real…"

"Yeah, none of this *feels* real either."

"You already fucked him, Chloe? I just don't understand," she shook her head again, before looking back at me. "Does Matilda know?"

"No!" I yelled. "God, no!"

"Well, damn woman. Sounds like you've got an adventure ahead of you."

"Yeah, I guess so," I said.

"Big dick?"

"God, Marie! Is that all that matters to you?" I laughed.

"Most of the time, yes, yes it is," she nodded. "So?"

"Yeah," I replied, a slow, secret smile spreading across my face as Bear's beautiful cock flashed in my head. "It's *huge.*"

Her squeals rang in my ears and I reached for my wine glass, pouring it down my throat.

What the hell had I gotten myself into?

Chapter 4

"Mom, maybe you shouldn't mix whiskey and xanax," I warned.

"You know flying makes me anxious," she dismissed me with a wave, her blonde hair shining under the overhead light of the front cabin of Bear's airplane.

He'd sent a private jet for us.

Mom was just as shocked as I was when she saw it and I could have sworn I saw goosebumps pop up on her arms when the pilot welcomed us aboard. My stomach was doing flips as I walked up the stairs and I exhaled with relief when I saw that Bear wasn't there.

The pilot welcomed us, told us to make ourselves at home and that Mr. Dalton would be waiting for us at JFK. I was grateful for the extra time before having to face him again. I'd been a nervous wreck since I'd left my house that morning.

Having an entire luxury jet at our disposal wasn't half bad, though.

"This is amazing," I said, letting Mom off the hook for mixing booze and drugs. It was her life to ruin and I had to assume she knew what she was doing.

Normally, I might have harped a little longer, but I was distracted by the sheer luxury of Bear's plane. The buttery soft, heated leather seats seemed to wrap around my hips and I melted into their warmth. Everything was shiny, new and probably cost more money that I could even imagine.

"Can I get you anything else?" The male flight attendant, Brody, and the pilot, Dawson, were the only staff we'd seen so far and they'd both been perfectly hospitable. The fact that they were magazine gorgeous was an added bonus. Tall, dark and handsome, they were easily the prettiest things on the plane.

"No, thank you, Brody," Mom said, flashing him a professional smile. She was impressed, I could tell, but she was doing her best to appear aloof and comfortable. If I had a nickel for every time she'd told me appearances were everything than I'd be rich myself.

Brody walked away with a curt nod and I couldn't help but let my gaze fall to his tight black slacks. They fit him like a glove, his tight ass perky and taut. I bit my lip as I watched him disappear behind a curtain at the front of the plane and sighed.

A week had passed since I'd seen Bear—correction—*fucked* Bear, and I still couldn't shake the feelings he'd stirred up in me. Tense and anxious, I'd been on edge the entire week. Despite the strong temptation to pick up the phone, I'd managed to make it through the week without calling him and asking him exactly what he expected of me.

After talking to Marie about it, I was looking at things a little differently.

I was determined to use it as an opportunity.

An adventure, like she'd said.

Maybe I wouldn't make any professional gains, but I was sure I'd be gaining something a little more valuable. Like life experience. Knowledge. Toe-curling sex.

I'd always felt like I'd missed out on so much. I mean, what did I have to lose, right? If New York sucked, if Bear turned out to be too much for me to handle—all I had to do was come back home to Portland.

An old friend of mine told me that she spent a year saying 'yes' to everything. She'd done things she never would have normally done. One of her little 'yes' adventures took her to Italy, where she ended up meeting a charming guy that swept her off her feet. As soon as she started saying yes, her life blossomed.

That's what I wanted.

I wanted to blossom.

I would do that. I would say yes to everything that crossed my path in New York and see where it took me.

The whir of the engine vibrated through my seat as the plane took off, my stomach flying up into my throat. I was a bundle of nerves, but it felt so fucking good. My chest was heavy and full with anticipation, leaving me breathless as I thought of all the things that might happen. The things I wanted to happen.

Sure, I'd hated New York when I visited. But maybe I just didn't have the right experience. Maybe I didn't say yes enough.

Loud banging noises sounded under our feet as the pilot pulled the landing gear up. I inhaled deeply, doing my best to relax my shoulders. I desperately needed to get a grip on myself. It was going to be a long few hours and Mom could usually see right through me. If she put her own anxiety aside for a few moments, she could easily figure out how tense I was.

"Bear assured me the corporate apartment would have everything we need," she said, looking down at her perfectly manicured nails. I shuddered at the sound of his name. "Our things should be delivered in a few days."

"I know, Mom," I said, rolling my eyes. "You already told me that three times."

"I like to be thorough, you know that," she said.

"Yes, I do," I sighed.

"I still don't understand," she murmured.

"Understand what?" I asked, stalling. I knew exactly what she was about to say.

"Why you changed your mind?"

"Mom," I replied, rolling my eyes again. She hated it when I did that and I knew it, but usually it was enough to make her stop questioning me. "We talked about this. He offered me a job."

"It's just that you were so adamant about not being in New York," she said.

"I changed my mind," I shrugged. "Maybe I was too hard on New York before. Marie loves it there. Maybe I just need to give it a second chance."

"Are you sure that's all?" she said, squinting her eyes over the whiskey glass as she took a sip.

"Yes," I said simply, smiling.

"Okay," she said, relaxing. I breathed a sigh of relief. I needed her to believe me. "I really think you're going to love it, sweetie. Our apartment is right across from Central Park and everything you'll need is within walking distance. Maybe we can get a dog?"

"What? A dog? Why?" I asked. Having a dog was never something Mom had time for before.

"Well, so you'll have something to do and someone to keep you company," she said. "I'm going to be spending most of my time at the office."

"So, what's new?" I thought, hoping I didn't sound bitter. I'd basically raised myself and I'd been just fine without a dog. I mean, I loved dogs but she'd always refused when I'd asked for one before.

"Look," she said, reaching over and putting her hand on mine. "I know I haven't been the most present mother in the world, but I'm always here for you, you know that, right? You can always tell me anything, Chloe. If you ever need me, especially now that we're going to be in this big city all by ourselves, all you have to do is call, okay?" Her grass green eyes peered deeply into mine and I wondered what she saw in them. We'd always had a frighteningly close psychic connection, despite the cold distance between us, and I knew she had to feel something was different with me.

"Of course, Mom," I said, patting her hand. "I love you. Everything's going to be great. Don't worry."

"You're right," she beamed back at me. I'd never seen her so happy. "It really is! I think this position is going to be the best job I've had so far. Bear's offer was so generous and he's been nothing but kind. I can't wait to get in there and roll my sleeves up. I think I can be a real benefit to him."

"He's lucky to have you, Mom," I said, leaning back in the soft seat and looking down at the fluffy white clouds out the window, Bear's face flashing in my head. My nipples hardened as I shivered and crossed my arms over my chest.

"Thank you, Chloe," she said, taking another sip of whiskey and leaning back and closing her eyes. "I think I'm going to take a little nap. I didn't sleep a wink last night, I was so anxious."

"Get some rest," I whispered. She was asleep in minutes.

I was lost in my own thoughts when I felt a tap on my shoulder a few minutes later.

"Ms. McDonnell?" Brody whispered, holding out a plain white envelope to me. "This is for you." He nodded as I took it from him and walked away without a word.

I looked over at my sleeping mother before quietly tearing open the side of it and sliding out the heavy folded paper inside. I unfolded it and a shiver ran down my spine as I read it.

Dearest Chloe,

I trust you have everything you need on the plane. Brody and Dawson will take excellent care of you and Matilda. I'm looking forward to seeing you soon. I'll be waiting when you land.

All My Best,
Bear

P.S. Remove your panties before you land.

Chapter 5

It was like something out of a movie.

Bear stood at the side of the sleek, black limo, a confident smirk on his incredibly handsome face as he watched Mom and I descend the stairs of the plane.

Night had fallen and a full, bright moon hung heavy in the sky, lighting our way as we walked towards him. The evening breeze was cold, hardening my nipples and brushing against the bare skin under my skirt.

Would he know that I'd followed his instructions?

A hot red flush washed over me as he took my hand to greet me, a brush of his lips on the back of my palm sending shockwaves through my body. He turned and greeted Mom exactly the same way.

I was convinced I would be able to feel this whole thing out as soon as I saw him again. What happened in the restaurant seemed like a million years ago, in a way. Desperately, I wanted to get him alone again, to see what he would do, to see who he would be now that I was here in New York.

"Welcome to the Big Apple, ladies!" he said, throwing a grand sweeping gesture across the skyline behind him. "Home of dreamers, freaks and unlimited opportunities!"

"Thank you, Bear," Mom gushed, her eyes smiling with excitement. She'd slept the whole flight and she now looked completely refreshed and ready to take on the world.

"My pleasure, my pleasure," he said. "Hop in and I'll take you to your new apartment!"

Mom slid into the back of the limo first and I paused before following her, throwing a quick look over my shoulder at Bear. He flashed me a smile and pressed his hand into the small of my back for the quickest instant and then it was gone.

But it was enough.

That one soft brush of heat sent shivers of pleasure through me, flipping a switch inside of me and turning that constant tingling sensation back up to ten. My breath caught in my throat as I slid in next to Mom. Bear followed, sliding into the seat across from us.

The limo was just as luxurious as the plane, with soft black leather seats and a full bar gleaming invitingly in the corner.

"It's so great to see the two of you," Bear said, his warm, deep voice as soft as velvet.

"You too, Bear," Mom said.

"Y-yes," I replied, hating that my words stuck in my throat immediately. I lifted my chin, determined to remain confident and calm. "Thank you, Bear."

"Drinks?" he asked. "Whiskey? Wine? What can I get you?"

"Sure, whiskey sounds great," Mom said. I threw her a glance as Bear grabbed a bottle from the bar and she grimaced back at me.

"Sure," I replied, cocking my head as I shot a daring glance back at Mom. "Whiskey, please."

Bear handed the glasses to us and sat back with his own.

"So, Matilda, your office is all ready for you to get started whenever you're ready."

"I'll start tomorrow," she nodded firmly. I resisted the urge to roll my eyes at her eagerness.

"Excellent," Bear nodded. "I've taken the liberty of hiring an assistant for you. I believe he'll be a great fit for you but don't hesitate to find someone else if necessary."

"I'm sure he'll be just fine if you chose him," Mom replied.

"I'm not always right," he laughed. "Ask my ex."

Silently, I stared across the limo at him, studying him, searching his every move for information. I was hungry for him, in so many ways. He intrigued me beyond belief. I wanted to know everything there was to know about him, I wanted to know what made him into the man he was, the kind of man that thought he could manipulate the world to his liking in such a confident, take no prisoners kind of way.

At the mention of an ex, though, I felt a sharp pang of jealousy. It was absurd, I know, but there it was. Hot, stinging and only increasing my hunger for knowledge even more.

"Chloe?"

"What?" I asked at hearing my name. I'd drifted off while staring at him like a school girl in awe.

"I asked if you're excited about the move," he said. His eyes were peering so deeply into mine, I felt hypnotized, mesmerized by the same darkness that had haunted me for the last week.

"Excited?" I parroted. "Yes, of course. Very much so."

"Wonderful," he nodded slowly, smiling, his perfect white teeth gleaming in the darkness of the limo as his gaze trailed up and down my body. I was hoping the smile he gave me as he met my gaze again held approval. "I'm glad to hear that. I have a perfect job lined up for you. I think you'll be very pleased."

"Oh?" Mom asked. "I'm dying to hear all about it. I know Chloe is too. Aren't you, Chloe?"

"Yes, of course," I responded, my eyes glued to his gaze. I swallowed hard as he let the silence fill the space between us, his eyes dark and teasing.

"Well," he said after a moment, "I'm still working out the last few details and I don't want to say anything just yet, but it's going to be huge," he winked. "All will be revealed in time."

"I see," Mom nodded, her smile frozen in place. "Chloe will need a little time to acclimate, but I'm sure it will be wonderful."

"Yes," I replied. "Thank you, Mr. Dalton."

"Chloe, please call me Bear. Mr. Dalton feels so formal."

"Bear, yes, thank you," I nodded, reminding myself to breathe, as I broke his gaze. I couldn't take it for long. It was so invasive, as if every time he looked at me, he was crawling right under my skin, burrowing into my mind, reading my thoughts.

I looked down at his hands and felt a hot blush creep up my neck. My mind flashed to the images that had been dancing around in there for days — Bear's hands on my hips, his cock pressing into me from behind as I lay splayed out on the table, his for the taking, his fingers tangled in my hair as he pulled my head back, his mouth brushing against my ear as he whispered those filthy words to me.

The limo slowed down and I looked out the window, my eyes traveling up for miles as I took in the huge glass skyscraper we'd pulled up in front of.

"We're here!" Bear said, as the driver opened the door. I stood on the sidewalk and lifted my head in awe. In Portland, there's a law that buildings can't be any taller than forty stories. Obviously, New York didn't have any such law. I'd never seen a building so tall.

"It's so big," I whispered. "How tall is it?"

"Sixty stories," Bear stood next to me, staring up at it with me, before leaning over and whispering in my ear, his lips barely brushing against my skin.

"Beautiful," he whispered. I turned to look at him and he smiled down at me. "Isn't it?"

"It is," I agreed.

"I designed it," he said, his eyes shining with pride.

"Oh!" I replied.

"It's a masterpiece, Bear," Mom said. "You should be so proud."

"I am, thank you, Matilda," he said, bending his head. "Let's go in!"

"Mr. Dalton, good evening," the doorman said. He was dressed in a double-breasted suit with braided gold trim and tassels hanging from the shoulders, his hands covered in white gloves.

"Jimmy, thank you," Bear said.

"This is Matilda McDonnell, my new CFO, and her daughter, Chloe. They'll be in the penthouse."

"Nice to meet you," Jimmy said, nodding and smiling. "Please let me know if there's anything you need."

"Thank you, Jimmy," Bear said, shaking his hand. When he pulled away, Jimmy discretely shoved the hundred dollar bill in his pocket that Bear had slipped him and opened the heavy glass doors for us.

The lobby was incredibly posh, with shining white marble as far as the eye could see. Low slung white leather couches and gleaming glass and chrome tables filled the space, a huge abstract painting hanging over a roaring stone fireplace.

Bear led us to the elevator, waving at the man behind the security desk along the way. Once the elevator doors closed behind us, he pushed the penthouse button on the panel.

"Hope you don't mind being on the top floor," he said to Mom.

"Of course not," she said.

"You have good taste, Matilda. I can tell you're going to fit in the city just fine!"

Mom laughed and took a deep breath.

"I can't believe we're finally here!" she said. "I'll find us an apartment as soon as possible, Bear. Thank you for letting us use the corporate apartment until then."

"Don't be absurd. You can use it as long as you like. You might find you want something a little farther out of the city after a while, but until then, consider it part of your salary, Matilda."

"You've been so generous," she replied.

"Well, I plan on getting my money's worth out of you, don't worry," he teased.

"I'm worth every penny. You know that," she replied.

I stood in the back, watching them through a maze of mirrors created by the four mirrored walls that lined the elevator walls. I could see Bear from every angle, all at once. It was like the thoughts in my head had somehow exploded into the atmosphere. I'd been swimming in thoughts of him for days now, and it was all too much.

I exhaled in relief when the doors opened.

"And here we go! Ladies first," Bear said, holding the elevator as we walked out into the most beautiful apartment I'd ever seen. I glanced over at Mom and she looked downright blissful. My eyes swept over the place and I realized just how perfect it was for her.

It was modern and swanky, in a minimalistic kind of way. The furnishings were a mirror of the ones in the lobby, all white leather and gleaming glass. The view from the private terrace was incredible and sweeping, making the city below seem almost far away.

It took us five minutes to walk through the five bedrooms and six bathrooms, the office, the kitchen and the den, with fireplaces in every room except the bathrooms. I couldn't help but smile at Mom's reaction. Whatever happened, whether I stayed or not, I was glad I was here to see this. She'd worked so hard after Dad left and she rarely stopped. I was happy she had a such a wonderful place that she loved to come home to.

"So, what do you think?" Bear asked. He seemed pleased with himself.

"Did you design the rooms, too?" I asked.

"Partially. I used an interior designer for the details," he said.

"It's perfect, Bear. I can't thank you enough," Mom said.

"No more thanks needed," he said.

"So, Chloe, which room do you want?" Mom asked.

"I was thinking —," I began.

"— Oh, no, Chloe will be staying at a different apartment," Bear interrupted.

Mom and I both looked at him in shock.

"What?" I blurted.

"Well, you're an adult, Chloe, I didn't think you'd want to live with your Mother. I arranged for separate accommodations."

"Oh," I replied, speechless. "But there's so much room here."

"Yes," Mom said. "There's no need for the expense of an entirely separate place."

"Nonsense," Bear replied. "Money is no object. I own so much real estate in this city, I couldn't fill it all if I tried. I'm sure Chloe would like her privacy."

"But —," I protested.

"—But nothing. It's already done," Bear insisted.

"Okay," I replied. "Thank you."

"You'll be a few blocks away. The building is a little less modern, but I think it'll suit your needs and give you a true taste of the city."

"That's so nice of you, Bear," Mom said.

"Y-yes, it is," I replied. My stomach was in knots.

Bear continued, "I'd like to take you there now. Do you mind if I show Chloe around the neighborhood?"

"I don't mind," Mom replied, shooting a worried glance at me. "If it's okay with Chloe?"

"Yes, of course," I replied, anticipation ripping through my veins. I'd finally be alone with Bear and I could hardly breathe just thinking about it.

"Excellent!" Bear replied. "Take your time to settle in Matilda. If there's anything you need, I've instructed the front desk to take care of you. I've also taken the liberty of booking you a hot stone massage. I find it to be a fantastic way of relieving stress, and I know the effect flying has on you."

"Thank you, Bear," she replied, still sounding a bit anxious.

"Shall we?"

"S-Sure," I stuttered, anxiety washing over me. I was so frustrated with myself. I wanted to appear the sophisticated young woman, ready to face New York and Bear with all the self-assurance that I was sure he expected. Instead, my hands were shaking and my palms were sweaty… and I was sure he could see my hard nipples beneath my clothes.

When his hand touched the small of my back again to lead me to the door, I froze. I took a deep breath and said goodbye to Mom, promising I would call her later, and then there we were, all alone in the elevator.

His hand remained on my back the entire ride down but he didn't say a word to me. We stood staring straight ahead into the mirror, the two of us side by side, the heat of his fingers searing into my skin as I struggled to breathe.

The image engraved itself into my memory. Me, trying to look professional with my tight pencil skirt hugging my hips. And Bear, to my right, towering over me, his expression relaxed and serious, his handsome face almost too much to bear. I wanted to turn to him, ask him a million questions, kiss him, touch him, beg him to slide his cock into me again.

"You didn't have to get me my own apartment," I finally said, my voice finally calm and soft, a stark contrast to everything screaming inside of me.

"Yes, I did," he said, his voice just as calm and cool as mine. The elevator slowly came to a stop, the doors opening smoothly as he leaned his head down and brought his lips right next to my ear. He dropped his voice to a low, grumbling whisper. "We're going to need our privacy."

My lips parted and a tiny sigh escaped my mouth as his hand pressed me forward out of the elevator, through the lobby and back into the waiting limo. This time, Bear sat next to me, his muscular thigh pressed against mine. He leaned forward, pressing a button that lowered the glass between us and the driver.

"262 Central Park West," Bear said. The driver nodded and the tinted glass rolled back up, leaving us alone.

"I think you'll enjoy living on the other side of the park, Chloe. Everything you'll need is within walking distance." His voice was low and velvety and I stared into his dark eyes.

"What about you?" I asked.

He raised an eyebrow and a slow smile spread across his face.

"I live nearby, and my office is five blocks away. I'm keeping you close."

I nodded, trying to figure out how to form the questions wildly spinning in my head. He put a warm hand on my bare knee and a shiver of pleasure ran through me.

"I trust you followed my instructions?" he asked.

"Instructions?" I asked, bewildered.

"Did you not receive my note on the plane?"

My face flushed with embarrassment when I realized what he was talking about.

"The note," I nodded, doing my best to meet his piercing gaze. A flush of embarrassment blossomed on my cheeks. It took all my strength not to look away.

"Yes, I did what you asked…"

"Good girl," he said, patting my knee, before sliding his hand further up my leg. My eyes widened in surprise. We were alone, but the driver was right there just a few feet away. Not to mention the millions of New Yorkers just outside the window. His hand was so warm and my legs were so cold and the sensation of his warmth sliding up my thigh was quite possibly the most delicious, welcome touch I'd ever received.

Slowly, I spread my thighs further apart as his hand traveled closer and closer to my bare pussy. The entire time, he held my gaze, his eyes widening with surprise as I opened my thighs to him.

Every fucking thing about this man was white-hot. The heat rolling off his body, his searing hands, his piercing gaze that locked me into it like he was putting me under a trance. My body flushed with heat as his fingertips grazed my lips lightly. He turned his hand, his palm pressing flush up against my quivering center.

I gasped, my lips parting as he continued to hold my gaze. Slowly, he pressed his fingers forward, one of them sliding between my lips and discovering the slickness that had threatened to fall down my thighs from the moment I read his note earlier. Another eyebrow raised and a slow smile of approval and then in an instant, he slid inside of me, a low moan escaping from my mouth.

"Is that for me?" he growled.

Speechless, I nodded as he sunk his finger in deeper, pulling out slowly and then plunging two back in. And then, just like that, he pulled away. I suppressed a whimper of protest, biting my lip hard instead.

"Good girl," he smiled, bringing his fingers to his nose. He inhaled deeply as another hot flush washed over my face. I couldn't believe this man. And just when I thought he couldn't shock me anymore, he pushed his fingers forward, sliding them between my open lips and twirling them over my tongue. Just like he'd done in that room at Departure.

"Mmmm," he murmured, "see how delicious you are?"

His fingers slid out of my mouth and I stared at him in awe. *The balls on this guy,* I thought. He was audacious and arrogant, daring and dangerous.

I fucking loved it.

He sat back in his seat as the car slowed to a stop in front of another apartment building, an older brick building not nearly as tall as the first one.

"We're here," Bear said, smiling at me as if he hadn't just had his fingers inside of me.

"Wow, it's awesome," I said, trying desperately to compose myself. "I can't wait to see inside."

"Let's go in," he said. "But Chloe?"

"Yes?" I asked, turning back to him.

"Pull your skirt down before you get out. You don't want to show all of Park Avenue what we've been doing."

My eyes shot down to my lap and I quickly pulled my skirt down, hiding my exposed flesh. His laughter was low and deep and I flashed him a quick smile, even though I wanted to die from embarrassment.

He leaned over and brushed a quick kiss on my cheek before the door opened and we stepped out.

"Shall we?" he said, offering me his arm. I put my hand on his arm and let him led me inside, my face hot and flushed, my pussy quivering.

Chapter 6

"It's so cozy," I said, as we walked into my new apartment. First of all, I couldn't believe how gorgeous and comfortable it looked, but secondly, I couldn't believe I was going to be living here.

"It's smaller than Matilda's, of course," he said. "But I thought it suited you better."

"You guessed right," I said and I couldn't help but beam a huge smile at him. "I love it, Bear, thank you. You're very generous."

"I'm happy to have you here, Chloe," he said.

I nodded, unsure what else to say as I walked around the apartment. It was older but it was stunningly beautiful. Intricate crown molding lined the ceilings, tall windows opened the room up to the city outside and the huge rooms were filled with informal furnishings—casual slip covered couches and dark red patterned fringed Persian rugs covered dark hardwood floors. The kitchen was entirely renovated, but even with the modern appliances and cabinets, it still had a rustic, cozy feeling to it.

"I have a surprise for you," he said, coming up behind me. "Actually, I have lots of surprises for you," he added with a low laugh. "Come with me," he grabbed my hand in his and led me down a long hallway.

At the last door on the right, he reached out and opened it, flipping on the light switch as we walked in. I gasped in surprise.

"Bear!" I exclaimed, throwing a hand over my mouth.

"I'm sure you'll need other things but I thought this would get you started," he said.

"It's amazing," I said, walking in. He'd turned the second bedroom into a sewing studio. There were dress forms lining the wall and a few long tables, a very high-end expensive sewing machine on another table in the corner and bolts of fabric lining the walls. "I can't believe this!"

"I want you to be happy, Chloe," he said, smiling sweetly at me. "Your mother told me how much your fashion designs mean to you, and I want you to understand that coming here doesn't mean giving up on your dreams and desires. New York is a pillar of fashion, and in time, I hope that you are able to make an impact of your own in this city. If anything is missing, please let me know and I'll have it delivered right away."

"Bear, this...this is too much," I said, shaking my head. I was starting to feel a little weird about everything. I barely knew him and he'd gone out of his way to make me so comfortable.

"Nonsense," he said, with a dismissive wave. "It was nothing."

"It's not nothing," I said. "It's very thoughtful. This is incredible."

He smiled down at me, those eyes turning me to complete mush. What was happening to my life? It was like I'd been picked up and plopped into someone else's fairy tale.

"Come on," he said, grabbing my hand again and pulling me out of the studio. "I want to show you something else."

I let him lead me back down the hallway and watched as he opened another door.

"Here's your bedroom," he said. "Of course, you can change anything you like."

It was like something out of a magazine. The four-poster bed looked so soft and plush that I wanted to jump right in it. It was covered in a jewel-colored patchwork quilt and flanked by a matching pair of shabby chic farmhouse style tables. Hanging over the bed was a lovely painting of the outline of a naked woman under a large oak tree.

"I love it," I said, twirling around.

"Look at the terrace," he said, opening a set of French doors. "The city is still loud up here, but it's beautiful. You have a wonderful view of the park."

"Oh, my god!" I exclaimed, leaning over the stone wall and looking down. Central Park loomed below, a massive, sprawling, green oasis. "I can't believe I get to live here!"

I turned back to him and he was staring at me, his eyes sparkling with something I didn't quite recognize. I grew quiet, licking my lips as I waited for him to speak or do something. I was at a total loss of how to handle a situation like this. Fuck, I didn't even know what kind of situation this even was. I didn't know what I was supposed to do, how I was supposed to act, what he expected of me.

He reached out, gently pushing a strand of hair off my face as he stared at me silently. His eyes trailed down, raking over my breasts and back up again.

"Chloe, we should talk," he whispered. "Let's go back in."

I nodded, following him. He sat on the bed...*my bed*...and I sat next to him, my hands in my lap as I looked over at him expectantly.

"I'm sure you have questions. And most of your questions will be answered soon enough, don't worry."

I nodded, listening intently.

"First, you're going to need a safe word."

"What?" I asked, my eyes widening.

"Don't be naive," he said. "A safe word. You know what that is. I intend to push your limits, but I am not a monster. So, what will it be?"

"I - I don't know," I muttered, bewildered. "I've never had one before."

"What's your favorite kind of pie?"

"What?" I asked, confusion filling my eyes.

"Apple? Cherry? Chocolate? What is it?" he asked.

"Peach," I replied.

"Okay, would you like to use Peaches as your safe word?"

"I guess, I mean, sure, whatever, but Bear —," I began.

"—what?"

"Why do I need a safe word?"

"Darling Chloe," he smiled, peering right through me. "Because I'm going to fuck you like there's no tomorrow. In every position. In *every* one of these rooms. And the day after that, I'm going to do it again. We'll get into more detail as we go along, but the last thing I ever want to do is hurt you. So don't forget your word."

"O-okay," I said, my voice cracking, my body tingling at his words.

"And Chloe?" he said, reaching up behind my head and sinking his fingers into my hair, pulling softly.

"Yes?" I asked, my eyes wide.

"Test yourself. Push your boundaries. Don't use that word unless you really mean it. As soon as you utter it, everything comes to a full stop. And nothing happens again until I *say* it does. Do you understand?"

I nodded and he let go of my hair, sliding a finger down my chin. He leaned closer, his face inches from mine as he smiled.

"Now, there's one more thing," he said.

"Yes?" I asked.

"It's important that you do anything and everything I ask of you and that you follow instructions perfectly, no matter how strange it might seem to you. Do you understand?"

"I think so," I nodded.

"Good girl," he murmured, brushing a kiss across my lips. A bolt of electricity ripped through my body as he kissed me, but his lips were gone before I could kiss him back.

"Any questions?" he asked.

"Yes, a million," I replied.

"I don't have time for a million questions. You can ask me one right now," he winked, his handsome face wrinkling at the edges. I couldn't believe the things he was saying, the things he was saying he was going to do to me. Fuck, I could barely breathe looking at him.

"Is this my job?" I asked, finally.

His laughter roared through the apartment and he shook his head.

"Of course not. I'll find you a real job. You can consider this a fringe benefit," he said.

I nodded, still completely confused. Did he expect me to be a sex slave and work for him at the same time? Was I seriously going to go through with this? To be honest, I would have done just about anything he asked of me, safe word or no safe word. In fact, I couldn't imagine what we would ever need it for.

It's not like I was going to ask him to stop fucking me, for fuck's sake.

Such a request seemed like a joke right now. In fact, sitting on this bed with him, it was taking all my strength not to beg him to fuck me right this very second.

Turns out, begging wasn't required.

"Now," he said, standing up. I watched as he pulled himself up, standing in front of me and looking down.

His eyes flashed, full of hunger and desire. "Stand up, Chloe."

I obeyed, silently standing in front of him.

"Are you ready?" he asked, without waiting for an answer. "I like being in control. Until I say differently, it would be best if you do everything I say without hesitation."

That was my first clue that I might be in over my head. I could have strolled out of there and never gone back. It's not like he was forcing me. It wasn't even that he wasn't giving me a choice. But what he wasn't really giving me were explanations and that's what I was desperately seeking.

He'd told me answers would come later, and I could either trust that and trust him, or I could walk out. I glanced over at the door of the bedroom, the thought of fleeing flashing in my head.

"I barely know you," I muttered. "I'm so confused..." My eyes searched his for answers, but all I saw was darkness.

Maybe it should have scared me. But it didn't. It only increased the intrigue.

His fingers snaked into my hair again, pulling my head back as I looked up at him.

"And that's what makes this so exciting, isn't it? I've been dreaming about fucking you again for a week. You're all I could think about, Chloe. And right now, I'm tired of talking. Do you understand? I'll tell you everything you want to know. You have to trust me," he said, pulling my head back farther, his eyes peering into mine. "Do you trust me?"

"I - I think so," I whispered, tears stinging my eyes.

He smiled and nodded.

"Good girl," he whispered, letting go of my hair and putting both hands on my shoulders. "Now, turn around and let me see your ass."

"What!" I yelled, my eyes widening in shock.

He smiled, his eyes lighting up with a mischievous glimmer and shook his head.

"You heard me, Chloe," he spun me around and gently pushed me forward, my hands landing on the patchwork quilt on the bed, my ass in the air towards him. His hands grabbed the edge of my skirt, lifting it up slowly over my hips, exposing my bare ass.

"You did good getting rid of the panties. Don't ever wear them in my presence again. Make sure you follow the rest of my instructions just as efficiently." His hands ran over my ass cheeks hotly and I shivered at his touch. "Your ass is absolute perfection, do you know that, Chloe?"

I blushed, my heart pounding so hard in my chest I could feel the blood pumping through my veins. His hands pulled my ass cheeks apart and I gasped.

"Bear," I said, shaking my head.

"Shhh, this is just the beginning, Chloe," he said, his fingertip trailing around my entrance. "I intend to get intimately familiar with every single inch of you."

I whimpered as he pressed his fingertip forward, sliding into me.

"Mmmm," he murmured, pressing further and further into me until his entire finger was buried inside of me. "So tight, so hot," he said. "You know, my cock is going to feel so amazing buried inside of your tight ass."

I whimpered again and he leaned down, whispering in my ear.

"Have you ever been fucked in the ass, Chloe?" he asked.

I shook my head no and moaned as he pressed even farther inside of me.

"Good girl," he whispered. "I promise you'll love it."

In an instant, his fingers were gone and I was left bent over the bed, my ass in the air, exposed, vulnerable and bashful as a skittish deer.

When I heard the sound of his zipper, I bit my lip with worry. Was he going to fuck me now? His fingers had felt so amazing and now that he was gone, I felt nothing but empty and hungry and oh-so-fucking needy. Normally, I would have hated these feelings but now, with Bear, I was relishing in them.

Slowly, I was losing myself in my desire for him.

"Turn around," he demanded. I did so, turning and sitting on the bed, and coming face to face with his perfect masterpiece of masculinity.

His cock was stunning. Huge. Long. Hard. And pulsing with hunger.

Hunger for me. Hunger for my body.

My eyes shot up to meet his and I saw the hunger reflected there, too. My own hunger raged through me. I'd needed a man like him in my life for so long and I never really knew it.

I wanted him to take charge.

I wanted him to tell me what to do to please him, to please myself. I needed Bear Dalton and I needed all of him.

And most of all, I needed every fucking inch of his exquisite cock.

"On your knees, baby," he said, his voice a low growl of desire, as his pants fell to the ground. He stepped out of them quickly, kicking off his shoes and ripping his shirt from his torso. I licked my lips as I drank in the sight of his sculpted muscles.

He was like a dream.

My eyes trailed down his tight abs, pulled down by the thin line of hair that led directly to his treasure. My eyes locked onto his pulsing cock, licking my lips as I watched his fingers wrap around his shaft before offering it to me.

A perfect prize, a beloved treasure. And all mine.

Pleasure pulsed through my body, every inch of me tingling with sweet anticipation. I reached out, claiming my prize, first with my hand, wrapping around the base of his throbbing hardness and then with my mouth, sliding his velvety cock smoothly past my lips, my tongue twirling around it delightfully.

When I heard him moan in pleasure, it was like music to my ears. His cock filled my mouth perfectly, his hardness pulsing against my tongue hotly. I devoured him, working my hands and mouth in a symphony of movement until he was moaning over and over, his fingers sinking into my hair and guiding my head gently as he thrust his cock in and out of my mouth.

"Good girl, good girl," he growled, over and over, his cock swelling as it slid across my lips. I sucked, harder and harder, working my tongue around his shaft, pulling the head between my lips until he pushed me away. I fell back on my feet and looked up at him.

"I'm not finished," I begged, my lips wet and swollen with desire. He smiled down at me, the look in his eyes turning savage and raw.

"Neither am I," he growled, his eyes full of white-hot determination. His mouth crashed against mine, his kiss hot and hard. I melted into him, our tongues colliding and tangling together in a hot mess of unbridled lust and desire. His fingers found their way to my buttons, pulling open my suit jacket and pushing it over my shoulders. My white silk camisole tore to pieces as he ripped it from my body, tiny pearl buttons flying everywhere.

"Stand up," he commanded. I jumped to my feet and he unzipped the side zipper of my skirt, pushing it over my bare hips until I was standing in front of him wearing nothing but my heels and my black lace bra.

His kisses turned harder and harder until he pulled away, unfastening the front clasp on my bra until my breasts spilled out into his hands. His fingers found my nipples, squeezing hard until I cried out in pain.

A slow, evil smile started on his lips and spread to his eyes, highlighting the darkness that I'd seen there earlier.

He was sweet, he was generous, he was kind, but there was a prevailing darkness inside of him that did nothing but intrigue me and turn me on. Maybe I should have been afraid. Maybe I was putting myself in physical danger. But being with Bear stimulated everything inside of me—not just my flesh, but my brain, too. My head was racing with wonder and awe, never knowing what was coming next.

He kept me on the edge of the Universe with every stroke of his tongue.

This was the kind of relationship that I'd yearned for. This was the kind of sex that I'd always imagined. This was the fantasy that I'd been searching for.

A real man.

A demanding man.

A man that knew exactly what he wanted, how he wanted it and how to take it.

How could I not appreciate that? There were no games. No pretense. No uncertainty.

There was nothing but need and desire and the willingness to fulfill it.

I'd never wanted to be fucked so badly in my life. I'd never wanted a man to take me, to make me his, to use my body in whatever way pleased him…all because it brought me pleasure.

Sure, I was confused as hell, but I'd never felt so fucking alive in my life and all I could do was beg for more.

Gently his pushed me back onto the bed, hovering over me and pulling his mouth from mine as he looked down into my eyes, his cock inches from my waiting pussy.

"You're the most beautiful fucking thing I've ever seen, Chloe," he whispered, his voice thick with lust as he rubbed his cock over my clit. I squirmed below him, my body thrumming with desire.

"Bear, please," I said, lifting my hips, eager for him to be inside of me.

"Tell me what you want, Chloe," he said.

"I want you, please, Bear, please?" I begged.

"Say it, say the words, baby," he said, pushing forward, his cock pressing into me ever so slightly, too slightly. I whimpered, pressing my hips up again.

"Fuck me, please fuck me," I cried.

"Good girl," he growled, as his lips found mine. His cock slid inside of me smoothly, one long, deliciously satisfying thrust that sent waves of pleasure rocking through every inch of me.

"Yes!" I cried, tears of joy springing to my eyes as I finally felt what I'd been dying to feel for so long. "Oh, my god, yes, yes, yes!"

He kissed me hard, too hard, the metallic taste of blood stinging my tongue. My pussy quivered in the sweetest pleasure around his hardness, my body singing in joy and fulfillment as he began fucking into me over and over again. My thighs wrapped around his hips, my hands wildly running over his rippling flesh, his strength on full display as he hovered over me, his muscles flexing as he expertly pulled every ounce of pleasure from my flesh.

His perfect cock hammered into me, slamming fully into me, his body banging against my swollen clit, his delicious fullness ripping everything away.

There was no more shyness, there was no more embarrassment.

There was no uncertainty, no confusion.

As far as I was concerned, as long as this beautiful man fucked me in this incredibly forceful and gorgeous way, then he could do anything in the world to me he wanted.

Fuck my questions. Fuck my need to understand.

All I needed was Bear's body, Bear's cock, Bear's kisses. Those are the things I understood.

The rest didn't matter.

All that mattered was our bodies, fitting together perfectly, crashing together in a perfect crescendo of everything good in the world.

His kisses turned deeper, his hands touching all of me all at once, his scent, his taste, his song…all turning everything around me and in me into the sweetest pleasure I'd ever felt.

"Bear, Bear, Bear," I cried, as I opened myself to him, as fully as I possibly could. My thighs fell apart, my arms wrapped around him, welcoming him in, inviting him into the deepest parts of me, parts of me that even I hadn't seen for myself yet.

He fucked me with abandon, his eyes closed, his hips working against me like a two hundred pound fuck machine.

Quivering, shuddering, quakes of pleasure washed over me, my body exploding into a million stars of light as I pulsed around his hammering cock, relentlessly pounding into me harder and harder until he crashed over the edge with me, his body shuddering hard as his huge cock swelled inside of me and exploded.

"Chloe!" he called, my name echoing off his tongue like a battle cry as he came inside of me.

"Bear, yes, yes, yes!" I whispered, his warmth washing over me and in me, as he moaned and kissed me again, his tongue searching deeper and deeper as we clung to each other, my entire body tingling with pure joy.

I fell back on the bed, watching him, his face flushed, his sculpted body so fucking alive and beautiful that it almost hurt to look at him.

He shuddered and pulled out of me, the absence of his warmth so palpable I almost pulled him back in. A whimper escaped from my lips as I stared up at him.

He pulled his pants up, zipped them and turned away from me. I was naked, splayed out on the bed like a harlot, begging for more as I watched him walk towards the door.

"You're leaving?" I asked, my voice full of breathless dismay.

"You need time to get settled. One of my drivers will pick you up at nine in the morning to bring you to my office," he said, before pausing at the door and throwing a quick smile my way. "Don't worry, Chloe. We've only just begun."

And then he was gone, just like that. Leaving me alone in this strange city, this strange apartment, with all these strange feelings coursing through my limbs as I tried to make sense of it all.

In the end, even that was pointless. Sleep found me before any rational thought appeared.

Chapter 7

Max introduced himself as I walked out to the sidewalk the next morning. My new driver had been announced at exactly nine a.m. by the door staff, just as Bear had promised. Because of the insane bumper to bumper traffic, it took over half an hour just to drive the mile from my apartment to Bear's office.

I'd sat in the back of the limo, staring out at the people rushing by on the sidewalk and wondered what stroke of luck had occurred that had permitted me to be the one in the back of this limo, instead of one of the other women on the sidewalk.

I'd spent the entire night tossing and turning on the insanely comfortable mattress that was now my bed. After unpacking, I realized I just felt lost. I had no idea what I was doing letting some man, a virtual stranger, do such things to my body. My goodness, it felt amazing, it was magical, it was like being put in a trance or something, but how had this all happened?

It was too fast, too confusing, and I was left with so many questions.

What was my job going to be? Bear had left that one important thing totally unanswered, leaving me with a big question mark hanging over my head. I didn't even know what to wear, so I'd opted for another suit, this one a deep maroon that I'd paired with a pair of black kitten heels. And I'd left the panties in the drawer of the dresser, just as I'd been instructed.

I wasn't sure if the ban included tights, but since I was getting picked up and not one of the many people walking the cold streets of New York City, I left the tights at home, too, hoping my long heavy coat would keep my bare legs warm enough.

I was wrong, of course. I was fucking freezing, even with the warmth of the limo's heater blowing out hot air. My bare pussy was so cold I finally understood why men's balls rose back up into their bodies.

When we pulled up to the tower with Dalton Enterprises emblazoned above the door, I took a deep breath and tried to calm the nerves that were racing through my veins. I wondered if this was ever going to get any easier—seeing Bear—because up until now every single time had left me shaking and shuddering.

The limo door opened and I stepped out, thanking Max and walking inside. I walked to the security desk and told them I had an appointment with Bear Dalton. The security guard was young and handsome, his short black hair a stark contrast to his bright blue eyes.

"Yes, Ms. McDonnell, Mr. Dalton is expecting you. Go right up to the forty-fifth floor."

"Thank you," I said, smiling at him. If this had been any other day, I might have flashed a flirty smile at him. He was my type. Or, what my type had previously been. I'd never have imagined I would be interested in a man like Bear, but here I was. Maybe I didn't know what my type was after all.

After a quick elevator ride, the doors opened to a sleek, shiny, modern office. The receptionist was a young pretty brunette, close to my age, but she seemed to be infinitely more sophisticated than me.

"Mr. Dalton will see you now," she cooed, leading me down a long hallway and opening a door at the end of it. I stepped in and took a deep breath

Bear was on the phone, but he flashed me a smile and gestured that he'd just be a minute.

"Jeffrey, this can't wait any longer. I want the deal finished today. Tell them they give us what we want or we walk, understood? We don't have time to waste on this project."

I arched an eyebrow as I listened and looked around his enormous office. Apparently, he was just as demanding in business as he was with me. He hung up abruptly and turned to me. A slow smile spread across his face and he walked towards me, his arms open. He embraced me warmly, kissing my cheeks.

"Good morning, Chloe. Did you get all settled in last night?"

I blushed at his mention of the previous evening, flashes of him fucking me running through my head.

"I did," I replied.

"Good, good," he said, releasing me. He walked behind the enormous dark wooden desk in the corner and sat down. "Sit."

I obeyed, just as I had every time before, without thinking, without questioning.

"Is my Mother here?" I asked. She'd called me last night, just to make sure I was happy with my apartment and I was pretty sure she was on the verge of asking me to live with her, but to her credit, she didn't. I didn't want to fight with her, but I was glad I had my own place, I was grateful to Bear for setting it up.

I needed privacy, but I mostly needed time alone with my thoughts.

"She's not. She was here earlier, but she went to meet with our board of directors across town. She's wonderful, isn't she? She insisted on hitting the ground running."

I nodded and stared across the desk at him. He looked different here. More professional, a little more stressed.

His usually relaxed shoulders were drawn up, his forehead was wrinkled in concentration. And yet, somehow, he still exuded the utmost confidence. All of this only added to his handsomeness, of course. He was a man of many layers, this much was obvious. I found myself wanting to peel back every single one of them and inspect them, explore them, taste them.

"I have something for you," he said, pushing a small white box with a red bow across the desk towards me.

"Oh, you didn't have to —," I began.

"—Open it."

"Okay," I murmured, taking it from the desk and slowly untying the red satin bow. I pulled the lid off and pulled the tissue paper back. My eyes squinted in confusion as I reached in and pulled out the object. It was a small black rubber object, tapered at one end and adorned with a shiny, pink costume jewel on the other end.

"What is it?" I asked, turning it over in my hand.

"You don't know?" he asked, his voice full of amusement.

"No," I shook my head, turning it around and inspecting it from a different angle.

"Oh, Chloe," he laughed. "We are going to have so much fun together."

"I don't understand," I said.

"Darling, it's for that perfect, sweet ass of yours. It's a bedazzled butt plug!"

"Oh!" I said, dropping it back in the box as if it were on fire.

His laughter echoed off the walls and I blushed furiously.

"Don't be embarrassed, beautiful. You're going to become very well acquainted with that."

"I don't think…" I began, but my voice trailed off as my eyes crashed with his.

"What's your safe word?"

"What?" I replied. "Peaches."

"Good, don't forget that," he said, standing up and walking over to me. I stared up at him, waiting for some sort of explanation. "Remember, you don't have to do anything you don't want to."

"Okay," I replied, my voice soft and shy.

"Stand up," he whispered, taking the box from me and placing it back on his desk. I stood up, smoothing my skirt over my thighs.

"Come over here," he said, walking back behind his desk and sitting down. I followed him and stood next to him. He pushed his seat back and pointed to the space under his desk.

"Get under there," he said.

"What?" I asked, my voice lifting three octaves.

"On your knees, Chloe," he replied.

I stood there, looking down at him, my eyes blinking in confusion as I shook my head.

"I don't understand," I said.

"Now!" he barked. I jumped in surprise, but without further questioning, sure enough, my knees buckled and I sank to my knees in front of him.

"Good girl," he said, reaching over and caressing my cheek.

I tried to smile up at him, but it was more of a quiver of my lips. My nipples hardened and my body began shuddering as he pointed to the space under his desk again.

"Crawl under there," he said. I put my hands on the ground, crawling on all fours into the space under his desk.

"That's it," he said, pushing his chair back up to his desk until I was stuffed into the tiny space and staring at his expensively covered knees and crotch.

"Can you hear me?" he asked.

"Yes," I replied.

"Perfect. Now take out my cock," he said.

My mouth opened in shock. I hesitated briefly as I looked at the bulge between his legs and then, as if my hands had a mind of their own, I reached up, unbuttoning his belt and his slacks and slowly unzipping them.

Pushing the fabric of his slacks to the side, I reached into his silk boxers, pulling out his huge, throbbing cock. It felt like velvet in my hands and I stroked it slowly, watching in awe as it kept growing harder and longer before my eyes.

"Good girl," he said, his voice thick with desire. "Now, wrap your lips around it, Chloe. And don't stop until I tell you to. Do you understand?"

"Yes, Bear," I whispered.

"Good, good," he said, as I brought my lips forward, sliding them down his shaft. His moans seemed to wash over me, leaving me wet and hungry. His cock filled my mouth deliciously and I felt everything else disappear, once again, as I lost myself in the sensation of his fullness.

Until he picked up the phone and then I came crashing right back down to Earth.

"Sarah, can you come in here, please?"

"Be right there, Mr. Dalton," I heard the receptionist say.

I froze, my hands and mouth frozen in motion and shock.

"Did I tell you to stop, Chloe?" he said, his voice a low growl.

A deep hot flush rushing to my cheeks as I slid my lips back over his hardness. I heard the door open and footsteps come closer as I kept bobbing my head up and down on his massive, throbbing cock.

"What can I do for you, Mr. Dalton?" Sarah asked.

Did she even wonder where I was? Could she see me? Did she know I was under the desk with Bear's cock stuffed in my mouth?

He reached under the desk, his hands finding my head as he tangled his fingers in my hair and pushed my head down gently. I gulped hard, fighting to breathe without making any noise.

"I need to reschedule my meeting with Anderson this afternoon," he said. "Make it for next Tuesday."

"Yes, sir," she replied. "Anything else?"

"Yes, make dinner reservations for two at the 21 Club for tonight."

"Certainly, sir," she said. "Will that be all?"

"For now," he replied, his hands pushing my mouth down even more around the base of his cock. I struggled to stay silent, willing myself to breathe as his cock slid in and out of my mouth, my tongue twirling around it.

Finally, Sarah's footsteps faded away and I heard the door click closed. Bear groaned and slid his chair back, pulling his cock away as he did.

I stayed under his desk, staring up at him in shock.

"That was a test, Chloe," he said, smiling down at me. "Come out of there. You did great."

"Th-thank you," I replied, unsure if that was even how I should respond. This man had taken everything I knew to be true and turned it upside down. I crawled out and he reached out a hand to help me to my feet until I was standing face to face with him.

His lips crashed onto mine, his hands sinking back into my hair, pulling my head back as he claimed my mouth. His kiss was hard and urgent and fast. Within seconds, he was turning me around towards his desk and pushing me forward over it. He reached down, lifting my skirt over my hips and moaning.

"Good girl," he said, his hand landing a hard, stinging blow on my ass cheek. "No panties. If you're always this good at following instructions, you and I are going to get along famously."

I jumped as he hit me again, his wide, hot palm landing blow after blow on my flesh as I whimpered at his assault. My ass was burning and it hurt — a lot — but with each new blow, shockwaves of pleasure shot through my body until I was wiggling my ass in front of him, each blow promising a new wave of welcome pleasure. I'd never been spanked before, not like this, not with such force or with such urgency.

Bear growled at my enthusiasm, my nipples hardening like tiny pebbles at the sound of his pants dropping. When I felt his cock slide into my slick pussy, I melted into his desk, raising my ass even higher to give him better access. He fucked into me, harder and harder, his hips slamming against me as the force of his thrusts pushed me into the desk. Everything hurt and everything felt incredibly fucking amazing, all at the same time. I would have begged for more, if I had to. I would have done anything he'd asked, just to get him to fuck me harder.

I came, over and over, huge, rolling waves of pleasure endlessly shuddering through me as he had his way with me, his cock fucking into me with the strength of ten men until he was crashing over the edge with me, his cock exploding inside of me, his hot, thick cum splashing against the walls of my quivering pussy as he growled with animalistic pleasure, pressing hard inside of me as he finished.

He pulled out and I shook my head in protest.

"Stay there," he warned. He reached over my splayed out body and grabbed the tiny white box from the desk, pulling the butt plug out.

"No, Bear, I don't think —," I began.

"Shhh, Chloe. You're going to love this, I promise, darling," he assured me. I bit my lip, bracing myself for the pain and humiliation that I was sure was coming and putting my head down, closing my eyes. I heard the sound of his desk drawer opening and then felt his fingers. They were cold and wet and he slid one into my ass easily. "Now, listen," he said, as he worked another finger inside of me. "I've used plenty of lube. This won't hurt. In fact, you're going to be begging me to let you wear this every day after this."

"I have to wear it all day?" I cried, my eyes flying open as I looked over my shoulder at him. He smiled a small, satisfied smile at my shock and nodded his head.

"Yep. Today you do," he said. I moaned as his fingers slid deeper and deeper, creating the most deliciously sinful pain I'd ever felt. He leaned over me, bringing his lips to my ear as he whispered to me. "You're going to wear this all day. You're not going to take it out until I tell you to. Understood?"

"Yes," I nodded.

"Good girl," he said, removing his fingers and slowly sliding it into me until it popped into place, leaving only the shiny gemstone exposed. "That's fucking beautiful," he said, staring down at me still splayed across his desk, my ass bedazzled with a sparkling pink diamond covering the entrance. He wiggled it around and I moaned.

"Now," he slapped my ass, "stand up. Walk around."

I stood up, trying to adjust to the fullness of it. I pulled my skirt down and took a few steps away from him.

"How does it feel?" he asked.

"I guess it's okay," I murmured. I'd never felt more shy before in my life. Part of me wanted to pull this thing out of me and throw it at him, run away, tell him to fuck off and that I never wanted to see him again.

The other part of me couldn't get over how incredibly fucking amazing it felt.

Somehow, he'd managed to make everything he did to me seem like the most natural acts in the whole world.

He wanted me to suck his cock with someone else in the room? *No problem.*

He wanted to bend me over his desk and fuck me with the door unlocked? *No problem.*

He wanted me to make me wear a bedazzled bauble shoved up my booty for the entire goddamned day? *No problem?!*

Really?! What the fuck was happening to me?

Bear Dalton.

That's what.

He watched me carefully as I walked around, doing my damnedest to get used to having it inside of me as I walked.

It wasn't easy.

I was shocked it didn't fall out, first of all, but it was lodged so firmly up there it didn't appear to be going anywhere. I kept my knees close together just in case.

Suddenly, images of being in public with this thing and all the ways it could go wrong filled my head. I turned back to him to protest, but the sudden movement sent a bolt of lightening from my butt to my clit and then straight to my brain.

I moaned, shivered and almost melted to the ground.

"What the hell," I cried, with breathless dismay.

He laughed lightly, his eyes wrinkling up at the corner and my stomach flipped.

Fuck, he was hot.

Fuck, this is weird, I thought.

Say yes, Chloe, I reminded myself. That's the promise I made to myself earlier and if there ever were one of those things that I might regret not doing later, this was it.

I had a slightly panicked thought as I wondered how I was going to get it out later, but I pushed the thought away. I wasn't the first person in the world to wear one of them, surely it couldn't be that hard.

At least I hoped not. A quick flash of myself at the emergency room complaining of a trapped bedazzled My Little Pony butt plug in my ass shot through my head and I opened my mouth to protest again.

"Sit down," he demanded. I hesitated, wondering if that was even possible. I went slower this time, much slower, wobbling over to his desk like a penguin.

"Do I really need to sit?" I asked.

He smiled softly and nodded.

"You'll be okay. Trust me." Trust him, huh? He wasn't the one with a unicorn up his butt.

I nodded, sitting gently in the chair in front of his desk, barely perching my ass on the edge. I sighed with relief when I realized it didn't hurt. In fact, I only felt it when I moved in certain ways and there was something mischievously forbidden about it. I sat down fully on it and my eyes shot open as the feeling went right to my clit again.

It felt so deep, so hard, and I knew I wouldn't be able to think about anything else the entire day.

"That's my girl. I knew you'd like it," Bear winked. "I have something else to give to you," he said, sliding a gold credit card across to me. I leaned over carefully, picking it up. It had my name on it.

"What's this?" I said, breathlessly.

"It's yours. Spend whatever you need to spend."

"On what?" I asked, shifting gingerly in my seat.

"On whatever you need, darling. Clothes, furniture, anything."

"Why are you doing this?" I asked, squirming.

"Doing what, Chloe?" he asked, his eyes smoldering as they stared deeply into mine.

He was so serious, so casual about this whole thing.

"Everything, Bear. The apartment. This credit card. The job, whatever it is…"

He cocked his head, staring at me thoughtfully before replying. The tension hung thick and heavy in the air between us.

I'd let this man touch me in places I'd never let anyone else touch. And he'd given me things I'd never imagined. And yet, I had no idea why in the world any of this was happening to me.

"The limo is waiting downstairs," he whispered, his low, smoky voice sliding over my ears like velvet. "Go shopping. Buy clothes. Lingerie, lots of it. Black is my favorite, and it would be in your best interest to please me, Chloe."

"You didn't answer my question," I prodded, swallowing hard with nervousness.

"No, I didn't," he smiled, standing up and walking over to me. "Tell you what. At dinner tonight, you can ask me anything you want, okay?"

"We're going to dinner?" I asked.

"Yes, didn't you hear me tell Sarah to make reservations? It's a very upscale place, so make sure you buy something appropriate. I'll pick you up at seven."

"Okay," I said, my head spinning. "But what about my job?"

"Chloe, this is your job."

"What is?"

"Beautiful," he said, leaning down and brushing a kiss across my lips. "Don't you see? It's your job to please me."

"So, I'm a glorified prostitute?" I asked, brazenly. A little too brazenly for someone with a sparkly pink butt plug shoved up their ass, actually. Bear wasn't fazed by it though. Instead, my boldness seemed to amuse him.

He smirked. "Of course not. I'm not paying to fuck you."

"Then what are you paying me for?"

"I'm not paying you. I'm taking care of you. Haven't you ever had anyone take care of you before, Chloe?"

"Not like this," I replied.

"Have you ever had a boyfriend, Chloe?" he asked.

"Yes," I replied, Harlan's face flashing in my head. I hadn't thought of him at all since I'd arrived. Hell, I hadn't really thought much of him at all since I met Bear. "He was awful."

"That's what I thought. He treated you badly, correct?"

"He was selfish and arrogant," I replied.

"Ah, a man after my own heart," he laughed. "Well, you see, Chloe, I want to give you more than that. Do I have my own selfish reasons for making you happy? Of course I do, I won't deny that. But it seems you need me as much as I need you."

"I don't need anybody," I said, raising my chin defiantly.

"You need experiences, Chloe," he said. "You need to live, don't you?"

"Yes, but —," I began.

"—then give me a chance," he interrupted. "Give me a chance to show you things you've never seen before. Give me a chance to show you what your body can do, to guide you into a world that you can only dream of. All you have to do is trust me."

He paused, smiling down at me confidently. He was so fucking handsome, so incredibly sexy, and maybe that's what it was, or maybe it was the fact that he'd already taken me to places I didn't even know existed within myself, but I couldn't help myself.

"You do trust me, don't you, Chloe?" he asked, his eyes peering so deeply into mine I thought I might never come up for air.

"Yes," I whispered. "I do." I had no idea why I trusted him, but I did.

The smile that he beamed down at me left me breathless.

"Wonderful!" he exclaimed, reaching for my hands and pulling me up from my chair. "You'll see, Chloe. This may not be what you expected, but it will be so rewarding in the end."

I nodded, speechless, still lost.

He kissed me again, pulling me close in a firm embrace before gently pushing me away.

"Now, go. You're making me hard again and I have a meeting in five minutes."

"Okay," I nodded. "But I can really ask you anything tonight?"

"Anything, beauty, I'm an open book," he said.

I took a deep breath, squaring my shoulders and nodding.

"Alright," I agreed. "I guess I'm off to go shopping."

"Good girl," he said. "Max can give you suggestions on where to shop. Buy anything you want."

"Thank you," I said, walking towards the door, the plug rubbing deep inside of me with every step.

"Oh, Chloe?" he said as I reached the door. I turned back, drinking in his sexiness one last time.

"Yes?" I smiled.

"Don't bother buying panties, darling. You won't be needing them."

My mouth opened in surprise and was met with his laughter.

"See you at seven!" he exclaimed, his eyes twinkling.

I turned away, shaking my head. I walked out to the reception area, avoiding Sarah's eyes the entire time, sure that she must know exactly what was going on under my skirt and doing my damnedest not to blush.

It didn't work.

Chapter 8

I walked out onto the cold New York streets, the wind and snow whipping around me, the frenzied rush of people speeding by so fast that I struggled to make it across the sidewalk to the waiting limo.

"Ms. McDonnell," Max nodded at me as he opened the door.

"Max," I said, turning to him before he closed the door behind me. "I need to go shopping, but I don't have any idea where to go. Somewhere upscale," I said, parroting Bear's words.

"For clothes, ma'am?"

"Yes," I replied.

"I know just the place," he smiled, before closing the door and running around to the driver's side. We pulled away from the curb and I leaned back in the seat.

My body had adjusted to the plug by now and the intensity of the sensation had lessened enough that with a little luck, I wouldn't make a fool out of myself. I couldn't believe I was doing this—going out in public like this. The entire situation was surreal.

I jumped when I felt my phone buzzing in my suit pocket. When I saw it was Marie, I smiled. She was exactly the person I needed to talk to.

"So?" she asked, not bothering with a greeting at all, just like always. "How's New York?"

"It's incredible. Bear's given me my own apartment, just off Central Park!"

"You aren't staying with Matilda?"

"Well, I thought I was going to, but no. Bear gave me my own place."

"How's everything going with him? Did he tell you what your job is?"

"Um…," I hesitated. "Well…."

"You fucked him again, didn't you?"

"Oh my god, Marie," I said, my words rushing out of me like a river, as I lowered my voice. I wasn't sure how much Max could hear through the glass panel separating us. "He's amazing."

"I'll take that as a yes?"

"Yes. Twice." She squealed and I pulled the phone away from my ear.

"I can't believe you're fucking your boss!"

"Neither can I," I said, smiling. "He's quite a gentleman, actually. When he's not fucking me, that is."

"He isn't a gentleman when he's fucking you?"

"Hardly," I scoffed. "More like a fuck machine. He's so dirty, Marie! He made me give him head while his assistant was in the room!"

"What!" she yelled.

"I know!" I said. "And… he gave me a gift."

"What kind of gift?"

"Marie, you won't believe this," I said, squirming as the plug sent jolts of pleasure through me.

"What is it?"

"Have you ever used a butt plug?"

Her laughter roared through the phone like a tornado.

"What! Sure I have," she said.

"Of course you have," I said. "I forgot who I was talking to."

"So he gave you a butt plug? What the fuck kind of gift is that? He's a billionaire, he should have given you diamonds!

"It does have diamonds. Pink ones, on the outside."

Her laughter was contagious and I couldn't help but chuckle.

"I'm wearing it right now," I whispered, hoping to hell that Max couldn't hear me.

"Now?" she cried. "What the hell? Where are you?"

"I'm in the back of Bear's limo on my way to go shopping. He also gave me my own credit card."

"Holy shit, Chloe! You hit the fucking jackpot!"

"I guess so," I replied.

"Why aren't you more excited?" she asked.

"I don't know," I sighed. "He's just such a mystery. He won't really answer any of my questions. I guess I don't have a real job, not that I can tell so far, except fucking him and doing what he tells me to, apparently."

"Look, I saw this man's picture, remember? Fucking him can't be that bad."

"It's not bad at all," I replied. "It's just not what I'm used to."

"Speaking of what you're used to, Harlan called me looking for you."

"Did you tell him I moved?"

"No. I didn't answer his call. He left a voice mail asking for information about you."

"Don't tell him anything. I'm avoiding him completely."

"I would, too, if I had a rich new sugar daddy," she laughed.

"Don't call him that!" I said.

"What should I call him, then? Your boyfriend?"

"No, I don't think that's appropriate either. I have no idea what to call him."

"Does he make you call him Daddy?" she laughed.

"Shut up! No, he doesn't," I said, laughing with her. "I just call him Bear."

"Well, whatever, I call him 'hot'," she said. "He must be a total freak in bed."

"That's an understatement," I said.

"So, wait a minute…you're going shopping right now and he's making you wear a butt plug the entire time? That's so…perverted."

"I know," I admitted.

"Does it feel good?" she asked.

"In more ways than one," I replied.

"Take a picture and send it to me!" she said.

"What! No, are you insane?" I asked. The car slowed to a stop and I looked out the window and saw that Max had brought me to Bergdorf Goodman's. "Marie, I have to go, I'm at Bergdorf's now."

"Bergdorf's! You bitch!" she teased.

"Eat your heart out," I said, so happy she'd called. Her laughter was the best medicine.

"Alright, alright. Look, Chloe, you deserve this. Let go. Enjoy everything. You only live once, you know. Don't be such a prude."

"I don't think being prude is an option at this point," I said.

"Good!" she replied. "Keep me posted. And um, Chloe?"

"Yes?"

"I wear a size seven in Louboutin's. Christmas is right around the corner," she reminded me.

I laughed and shook my head.

"Yeah, yeah," I said. "I'll call you soon. Love you!"

"Love you, too! Size seven!"

I hung up the phone feeling lighter than I had since I'd arrived in town. Marie always had that effect on me. Her perspective was always a little skewed but she managed to see the bright side of things most of the time.

I walked into the store, my step a little lighter, despite the pink ring pop stuffed inside of my butt. Another shiver of pleasure shot through my body as I gazed at the huge, golden Christmas tree shimmering at the entrance to the store.

I looked around at all the people rushing past me and grinned at my private secret.

I spent the rest of the day shopping, silently thrilled at my secret adventure, my body tingling with pleasure as Bear's face stayed front and center in my mind with each step, thanks to the plug.

By the time I made it back home to my apartment, I was exhausted and I'd put a serious dent in Bear's credit card.

I'd had five separate orgasms, in five separate dressing rooms.

Trying on clothes had never felt so fucking good.

Chapter 9

The view from my terrace was stunning. I sat at the little table out there, sipping wine and staring down at the tops of the trees in Central Park. Lights glittered around the city, sparkling like little diamonds adorning all the shops and cars and buildings. My neighborhood was bustling with activity and the energy that sizzled through it was exciting, but exhausting at the same time.

Bear was picking me up in an hour for our date and I was incredibly nervous. All of our interactions up till now had been quick and rushed. Sitting down with him over dinner was going to be a completely different experience. It would be intimate, in an entirely different way than having sex with him had been.

He'd texted me shortly after I'd gotten home today, giving me permission to remove the plug. I'd been so relived after wandering around with it all day and wondering just how long he would force me to wear it. Getting it out proved to be an adventure all its own but I'd finally succeeded after a few bungled attempts.

I'd gotten so excited taking it out, that I'd collapsed on my bed afterwards, my fingers bringing me to orgasm again. I'd been coming all day.

It was all too much. Too much physically, too much mentally. He'd managed to mind fuck me all day and he wasn't even there.

It was the most erotic thing I'd ever experienced. He'd crawled into my mind without me realizing it.

And yet, here I was, still going along with his games like an obedient puppy. If I had a tail, I'd be wagging it just as excitedly as any puppy would be, too.

It was obvious that Bear loved games. And now, it was apparent that I loved Bear's games just as much. The fact that he'd warned me that we were just getting started only added to the excitement.

I took a sip of my wine, the ruby liquid doing nothing to quell the nervousness running through my veins as I tried to imagine what Bear had in store for us tonight. Somehow, I knew he wasn't going to just stop at having a nice dinner together. So far, he'd been full of surprises at every turn.

My phone buzzed and I glanced down, sighing when I saw it was my Mother calling. I'd managed to get through the entire day without talking to her.

"Hey, Mom," I answered.

"Chloe, how was your day?" she asked.

"It was okay," I said, glad she wasn't here to see the blush that crept up my neck.

"What did you do?" she asked.

"Just a little shopping. What did you do?"

"I had the longest meeting of my life with the Board of Directors. Then, I went back to the office and met with my assistant for the rest of the afternoon to get things in order for the rest of the week. I'm giving a presentation on my proposals for the company on Friday. It's going to be a long, busy week."

"Sounds like you're right in your element," I replied.

"That's true," she laughed. "I loved every minute of it."

"I'm glad you're happy, Mom," I said.

"I am. Although, I have to admit, I'm not really happy with our living situation. It would have been much better to come home to you."

"I like my apartment. It's best we have our own space, Mom," I replied.

"I suppose so," she sighed. "But we have to promise to see each other as often as possible, okay?"

"Sure," I replied.

"How about tonight? Let's go find someplace to have dinner."

"Oh, I can't, Mom," I replied. "I'm having dinner with Bear."

"With Bear?" she replied. I could almost see her eyebrow raise through the phone.

"Yes, um…," I hesitated. "To talk about the position he has for me," I lied. The only positions I expected Bear to have for me included missionary and doggie.

"Oh, I see," she said. "Well, that's good. I hope it's something where you can use that degree of yours. I'd hate to see your talents go to waste."

"I wouldn't worry, Mom," I replied, blushing again as I thought about the new talents I was acquiring. Not everyone has the skills to wear a butt plug all day and I figured that had to count for something valuable later in life. "It's not like I'm going to work for him forever, whatever it is."

"That's true. It's good not to get complacent, Chloe. You need variety in your life. But at the same time, Dalton Enterprises is a wonderful company to work for. Bear's very generous. I'm sure he'll give you the biggest benefit package he has."

I spat out the wine I'd just sipped into my mouth and began coughing.

"Are you okay?" Mom asked. "Chloe?"

"I'm okay, Mom, sorry," I replied finally. "I should go get ready."

Suddenly, I couldn't handle talking to her anymore. Her questions, her talk of benefits packages—if she kept it up, she'd figure everything out very quickly. She was like that. That's why she'd come so far in her career—her instincts were fine-tuned and cat-like and she didn't miss a thing.

Being a teenager around her was a nightmare. Keeping secrets was out of the question. Now that I was an adult, the last thing I wanted was for her to figure out that I'm fucking her boss.

She would not be happy, not by a long shot. In fact, she'd be mortified.

I had to keep it together, for both of our sake's.

"Alright, dear, have a nice night. Let me know what kind of a job he gives you. Maybe we'll end up working together?"

"Okay, Mom, I will. Good night," I said, hanging up the phone with a sigh of relief.

I walked back in the apartment, turning on some music and pouring another glass of wine, before heading back to my bedroom.

I'd left all my purchases lying on the bed and as I sorted through them now, hanging the dresses and suits up in my closet and putting the delicate lingerie in the dresser, I imagined wearing all of this for Bear. I wanted to make him happy.

Bear had told me not to buy panties, but I had anyway. I couldn't endure an entire New York winter without wearing underwear, for fuck's sake.

After putting everything away, I put hot rollers in my hair and applied my make-up, my body finally beginning to relax a little with the wine. I needed it. I'd been on edge for days, unable to shake the feeling of being completely unsettled and disoriented.

It was like aliens had beamed me up and plopped me down on a different planet.

I didn't know this life. I didn't know this woman in the mirror, in fact.

I'd grown up doing my part to fight the patriarchy, a fierce feminist throwing up my fist with my fellow sisters. I'd marched in countless protests, fighting the powers that threatened to oppress us, which mostly was made up of old, white men. In fact, I didn't shave my legs the entire year after I turned eighteen; a silent, personal protest against the forced feminization of women. And I'd stopped wearing bras the year after that.

And now, here I was, subserviently obeying a domineering man like a goddamned Stepford wife and loving every fucking second of it.

Who was I? Where was the Chloe I thought I was? How could I have allowed Bear to have so much power over me?

Was I losing myself? Or, had I just finally found myself?

I was getting used to the constant questions swimming in my head. I was getting used to not having any answers to them, too. The confusion had become a permanent resident in my head, but maybe tonight I'd finally be able to break through them.

Bear told me at his office that I could ask him anything I wanted and I was looking forward to our question and answer session.

By the time my doorbell rang, I wasn't sure I wanted answers. Not knowing what was going on created an air of mystery to everything that had left me excited. Turned out, anticipation and adventure turned me on and I didn't even know it.

Maybe I was finding myself after all.

Maybe Bear was right about me.

I opened the door and damn near swooned when I saw him.

He was dressed in a sleek, black tailored suit, his hair slicked back and his dark blue eyes were shimmering with life.

"Hello, Beauty," he said, planting a kiss on my cheek.

"Hi," I replied, a jolt of shyness washing over me. I lifted my chin, determined to keep the shy, naive Chloe at bay tonight. I wanted to project the sophisticated, daring, mature Chloe instead.

I wanted to impress him.

"Would you like to come in?" I asked.

"My driver is double-parked. If you're ready, we should get going."

I pushed away a twinge of disappointment and nodded and smiled. He'd fucked me right away the last two times I'd seen him, so I just assumed he would do that again.

I guess this was a real date, after all.

"I'm ready," I replied. I grabbed my purse and keys, locked up the apartment and walked to the elevator with him. After a silent ride down to the street, he whisked me into the back of the limo.

"Would you like a drink?" he asked, the bright lights of the city swirling around us reflected in his eyes. I'd already had two glasses of wine to calm my nerves earlier and I was a light weight when it came to alcohol. I could hear Marie's warning in my head, my usual drinking partner.

"There's a reason we call you two-drink Chloe," she'd say. I pushed her voice away and smiled. The nerves were too much. This was definitely a three-drink night.

"Wine, please," I said, having the good sense not to mix the wine with anything else.

He poured me a glass and handed it to me and I did my best to sip it slowly. Taking deep breaths between each sip, I smiled over at him.

"How was shopping?" he asked.

"Max took me to Bergdorf's," I replied. "It was a lot of fun."

"Bergdorf's? How boring," he said. "I'll get you a list of better places."

"They had a huge golden tree and the place was a madhouse," I replied.

"It always is at this time of the year," he nodded.

"Did you get what you needed?" he asked, his eyes raking over the tight black dress I'd bought. I thrown a long camel colored cashmere coat over it and left it open. Thankfully, the limo was warm.

"I did," I said. "Thank you."

"You're welcome," he replied, his warm hand landing on my bare knee. Shivers of pleasure shot through me and I felt the wetness seep into my panties at his touch.

He smiled slowly and his hand began trailing up my thigh, pushing my skirt up with it. I moaned quietly as his fingers brushed against my bare skin.

"Mmm," he moaned approvingly. "Are you always this good at following orders?"

"Are you always this good at giving them?" I quipped.

He pulled his hand away and laughed.

"I guess I am," he said. "I'm not much for negotiating."

I smiled and pulled my skirt down over my thighs. He beamed back at me, then leaned over and kissed my cheek.

"You look incredible, Chloe," he said.

"So do you," I replied, my eyes trailing over his suit admiringly. It fit him like a glove, outlining the smooth muscles of his thighs, framing his wide shoulders perfectly.

Of course, in my mind, I was ripping that damned suit right off of him, remembering the perfect flesh beneath it. I was much more interested in his skin and everything under that. The rest was just for show.

"You're sweet," he said.

"Thank you," I replied, shrugging.

"Nothing wrong with being sweet," he said.

"I'm not so sure about that," I replied. "Ask my mother. Sweet isn't one of her most valued traits in a person."

He laughed and nodded.

"You obviously don't get your sweetness from her," he said.

"No, I don't," I agreed.

"So, where do you get it?"

"I don't know, actually. I wouldn't really call myself sweet, if you want to know the truth. Shy, quiet? Sure, but sweet isn't something I've ever strived for. In fact, I like to think of myself in fiercer terms."

"Fierce?" he asked, raising an eyebrow.

"Yes," I said, raising my chin, "Contrary to how I might appear to you, I'm actually a feminist."

"A feminist, huh?" he asked. "Of course you are. Why wouldn't you be? So am I."

It was my turn to laugh.

"What?" he asked. "You think just because I like to be in control, I can't be a feminist?"

"I didn't say that," I replied. "But since you brought it up, what exactly is the deal with you?"

He blinked, his eyes widening for a second before wrinkling up at the sides while he laughed again.

"Oh, Chloe, you do have questions, don't you?"

"So many," I smiled.

He patted my knee and brushed a quick kiss across my lips.

"Hold that thought," he said. "We're here."

The limo slowed in front of an old building with big iron gates surrounding a patio and a line of small jockey statues adorning the top balcony.

"Come on," Bear said. "It's a little fussy and the crowd is ancient, but they have the best steak in Manhattan."

We slipped out of the limo and he grabbed my hand as he led me inside like he owned the place.

Chapter 10

The restaurant was packed. Like something out of a movie, the lights were low and the entire place was surrounded by the dark wooden panels of the walls. And Bear was right—everyone in there, except the wait staff, appeared to be at least over fifty. I hadn't seen this much white hair since my Great Aunt Sally's funeral last year.

Unfortunately, the tables were insanely close together and all my dreams of asking Bear dozens of probing personal questions flew right out the door.

We were seated right away, because as soon as the maître d' saw Bear, he sprang into action. Bear pulled out my chair, waiting for me to sit down before sitting down himself.

We were seated between one very old couple on our left and a couple of businessmen deep into a discussion about the stock market on our right.

"Remember, we're here for the steak," Bear reminded me with a wink.

"I guess my questions can wait till later," I replied.

"We have all the time in the world, Chloe," he said, sending a shiver of electricity through my body with those piercing eyes of his. He was by far the handsomest man I'd ever seen, surpassing even my old go-to movie stars. George Clooney and Brad Pitt had nothing on this guy. "Let me order for you. You do like steak, right?"

"Yes," I replied. "I love it. Rare, please."

"Good girl," he said, flashing me a smile. I blushed, remembering all the other times he'd called me that.

My eyes trailed across the restaurant as he perused the menu and what a strange place it was. Dozens of old, vintage toys hung from the ceiling, which I thought was odd for such a fancy place. The waiters bustled around carrying silver platters and winding through the busy dining room. Glasses clinked and the low buzz of conversation created a frenzied energy that made it hard to relax.

Bear put down the menu and a waiter appeared immediately. I watched him order, lost in the way his lips formed the words and I couldn't help but anticipate when those lips would be on me again. When the waiter disappeared, I leaned over to him.

"Why are you single?" I whispered.

He smiled and shook his head.

"I'm a bit of a handful, if you hadn't noticed," he said.

"Still," I replied. "A man like you…rich, handsome…"

"You think I'm handsome?" he asked, striking a funny pose.

"You know you are," I laughed.

"Well, I could ask the same of you, Chloe," he said.

I shrugged, thinking of Harlan and immediately wishing that I hadn't.

"I'm newly single," I said. "Not soon enough."

"Ah, yes, the ex-boyfriend," he said, leaning back in his chair. "What's his name?"

"Harlan," I muttered. "But let's not talk about him."

"Okay, what would you like to talk about?" he asked.

I stole a quick glance over at the couple next to us. The old lady smiled and leaned over.

"You two are a very handsome couple," she said, her voice shaking as she caught my eye.

"Oh!" I replied, shaking my head, "we're not —."

"—Thank you, ma'am!" Bear interrupted. "I think so too!"

"Oh, you're quite welcome, young man. Treat her well, good women are hard to find!" she said.

Bear laughed, pouring on the charm.

"Don't I know it!" he exclaimed, before turning to address her husband. "Looks like we lucked out, Sir!"

"Oh! You!" the old lady admonished him, blushing slightly.

I sat there, smiling like an idiot, falling victim to Bear's charms, too.

When the waiter returned, he had a bottle of wine in his hands. He presented the label to Bear with a formal bow and I did my best not to giggle.

"Sir, as you requested. A 2006 Chianti Classico Riserva."

The waiter poured a tiny bit in a glass and handed it to Bear. He sniffed it and took a sip, nodding approvingly.

"That'll do, thank you," Bear said. The waiter poured the wine into our glasses and left the bottle on the table. I reminded myself not to drink too much again, wondering exactly how much that one bottle cost, at the same time. Probably a month's rent at my old place in Portland. I felt guilty wasting it, but hopefully Bear would drink most of it, because if I had anymore wine I was going to be sliding under the table in a drunken puddle of embarrassment.

"So, Chloe," he replied. "Let's talk about this job."

"Job?" I asked in surprise. I'd given up on thinking he was going to give me a real job and if he started talking about blow jobs and butt plugs in front of these people, I'd crawl under the table no matter how much wine was involved.

"Yes, I told you I was going to give you a job, didn't I? Did you not believe me? Besides, if I don't, Matilda will start asking questions, won't she?"

"She already has," I replied. "I just thought you said —," I began.

"—Something came up," he interrupted. "I think you'd be a good fit for it. It's a little outside the box, but I think you can handle it."

"Oh?" I asked. "What is it?"

"You're a fashion designer, correct? Well, I don't deal in the fashion industry, but I just bought a new hotel and I need an interior designer."

"You want me to be an interior designer for a hotel?" I asked, my heart speeding up at the thought of such a huge job.

"Sure, why not? I mean, it's not fashion, but I figure if you've got style then you've got style, right? What do you think?"

"Bear, I've never done anything like that before," I protested, shaking my head.

"That's okay, you'll learn. If you need help, we'll get you an assistant," he said, with a dismissive wave. He lowered his eyelids, the blue darkening in his eyes as he peered at me intently. "I have faith in you, Chloe."

"Th-thank you," I stuttered, my heart pounding so hard I thought it would burst from my chest at any second.

"You'll have a handsome salary, too, don't worry," he continued. "With a full benefits package, of course."

I felt myself begin to blush again at the mention of the benefits and smiled at him.

"My mother will be happy to hear that," I said.

"I thought she would," he winked, his handsomeness taking my breath away. "Of course, I hope you realize that this doesn't change anything about our previous arrangement. Everything we discussed earlier still holds."

"Oh, right," I said, my body tingling. "You don't think that's a conflict of interest?"

"I don't really give a shit," he said, the sternness returning, sending a jolt right through my spine.

"I see," I replied, sipping my wine again, trying once more to desperately hide the turmoil bubbling inside of me.

How in the world would I know how to design a hotel?

And yet, how in the world could I ever say no to him?

"Does all of that work for you?" he asked.

"Yes," I said, nodding, as I swallowed hard. "I mean, I still have questions…"

"Of course you do. And like I said, we have all the time in the world for questions."

Our dinner arrived at that moment and instead of asking my questions, I ate.

Gloriously, slowly, decadently…I devoured each and every scrumptious bite of what was indeed the best meal I've ever eaten in my life. The wine kept flowing and I abandoned my intentions of slowing down. By the time our meal was finished, we'd finished the entire bottle.

I didn't really feel it until I stood up to go to the ladies room. I made my way across the room, doing my best not to trip in my new Prada heels.

I need to find a way to incorporate some sturdy boots into my wardrobe if I'm going to be drinking like this, I thought, as I stumbled through the door of the ladies room and right into the most glamorous woman I've ever seen.

"Oh!" I slurred and stumbled back. "Excuse me!"

She'd been walking out as I was walking in and I ran right into her—my melting face doing a face plant right into her creamy, perfumed bosom.

Blood rushed to my face and I looked up at her. She was amazonian tall, looming over me in all her manicured perfection. Her long blonde hair flowed around her like a satin curtain, with shimmering waves of golden softness that looked like it would melt if you touched it. I resisted the urge to reach out and do just that. It looked as fine as cotton candy and yet there was so much of it. Once I finally made it past all the waves and looked into her face, I gasped.

Her eyes were purple. Elizabeth Taylor violet. I peered into them, drinking them in like I'd just seen a rare creature in the wild. Anger flashed through them like wildfire and I blinked and took another step back.

"Excuse me," I said again, stepping around her, my eyes quickly trailing down and taking in the rest of her. Her black sequined gown fit her sculpted body like a glove, outlining every curve of her lean frame. In Portland, we'd say she had a yoga body. But this creature was so perfectly put together, I couldn't help but wonder if some of it was man-made.

She was stunningly perfect.

But Mom always told me nobody was perfect. I walked past her and ran into the first stall of the luxurious lounge and wondered what this woman's imperfections were.

It didn't matter. I had plenty myself and the last thing I wanted to do was think about my own flaws right now, let alone anyone else's.

I needed to get my head together.

First things first, I'd had entirely too much wine. I took a deep breath, trying to gather my composure.

Second, these shoes were fucking awful. You'd think the fact that they'd cost a small fortune they'd be more comfortable than they were, but they weren't. They dug into my heel and caused the arch in my foot to cramp. I couldn't wait to get them off. I yearned for the comfort of my boots once again.

I stood up and stumbled out of the stall and over to the sink, shaking my head the whole time. I turned on the gold plated faucet and watched the water run out in a thin, smooth line. I couldn't help but muse about the fact that even the water seemed to flow better when money was involved. The sink in my studio back home sputtered and bubbled like a dying fish when I turned it on.

This new lifestyle was going to take some getting used to, but maybe it wasn't so bad at all. Being out with Bear certainly wasn't bad, either.

I looked up into the mirror and was shocked to see the woman still standing there. Leaning against the wall and casually checking her perfect scarlet nails, she looked up and smirked at me.

"I saw you with Bear," she said, raising an eyebrow.

"Y-yes," I replied, drying my hands and turning to her. "I'm Chloe," I said, holding my hand out towards her.

She looked down at my hand suspended in the air between us and snarled. She literally fucking snarled! I pulled my arm back down to my side and took a deep breath.

"I'm Zoe," she said. "Zoe Rothchild."

"Nice to meet you," I nodded, trying to muster a polite smile, despite her rudeness.

"You fuck him yet?" she asked suddenly, her violet eyes turning cold and hard.

My eyes widened in surprise.

"He's my employer," I replied, finally finding my voice.

"Oh, I see," she nodded, her eyes trailing over me as she sized me up. "So, not yet."

"Have *you* fucked him?" I asked, the wine shooting rare courage through my veins.

"Once," she quipped. "Let's just say he has certain peccadilloes that only appeal to a small audience."

I nodded, biting my tongue, despite the urge to say something, anything, to knock this woman off her high-horse. I hated her instantly.

"Just watch yourself, Chloe," she drawled, her lush red lips turning to a sickly smirk. "He may be powerful, handsome, and generous—but Bear Dalton is not at all what he seems," she warned.

"You seem like a nice girl," she shrugged, staring deeply into my eyes. "But be warned—Bear will eat you alive."

I had no idea how to respond. Luckily, I didn't have to.

She shook her head slowly before turning on her heel and walking out.

I exhaled and realized I'd been holding my breath the whole time.

Her words sliced right through me, sending a dagger of doubt right into my gut.

* * *

At my front door two hours later, Bear paused before walking in behind me.

"Aren't you coming in?" I asked, turning to him, hating that I'd slurred my words again.

"Not tonight, Beauty," he said, planting a gentlemanly kiss on my cheek.

"Why not?" I asked, disappointment rushing into my heart. I'd been anticipating being alone with him all night. Each time he raised his glass to his lips, a tiny shiver ran through my body as I imagined how his touch would feel later. I'd even set out the best negligee I'd bought on my bed.

"Two reasons, darling," he replied, his voice a low whisper in the hallway. "One, I have an early meeting in the morning. Two, you're drunk."

"I'm not drunk!" I insisted.

"Chloe," he smiled. "You're adorable and I really don't care if you had too much wine. I wanted you to have a good time tonight."

"I did!" I replied. "That was the best steak I've ever had in my life!" I was being a little too enthusiastic, but it was easy to blame that on the wine too. "But I really wanted was to spend some time with you," I said, reaching out and grabbing his tie.

I pulled him close, my lips brushing against his. He kissed me back tenderly, gently, so sweetly my heart swelled with emotion.

He pulled away, staring into my eyes as he reached up and grabbed my hand. He pulled it down, pressing it against his cock. It was rock hard, hot and throbbing in my hand, full of promise. My eyes widened in surprise and I squeezed gently, a tiny moan escaping from my mouth.

"Yes!" I whispered excitedly.

"No!" he insisted, backing away with a smile. "I just wanted you to feel how much I want you, Chloe. But not like this, darling." He brought his lips to my ear, whispering seductively. "The things I want to do to you right now require complete consent. You aren't capable of providing that right now and that's okay. But don't imagine for a moment that I don't want you, Chloe."

I smiled, nodding, as tears sprang into my eyes. I reached up, snaking my arms around his neck and hugging him close to me. He hugged me back, his massive arms so warm around me I could have melted into them forever.

I sighed as he pushed me away.

"You could just spend the night," I offered. "We don't have to do anything…"

His laughter echoed down the hallway.

"I'm not that strong of a man, Chloe," he said, shaking his head, his gorgeous eyes wrinkling at the corners. "I am only human, after all."

He kissed me again and then gently pushed me inside.

"Close the door and lock it," he ordered.

I smiled, stepping back into the apartment, my eyes glued to his. I didn't want him to leave, but I was beyond impressed with his manners.

"Goodnight, darling," he whispered, as I closed the door, my heart heavy, my head confused and five stupid words running over and over in my head.

'Bear will eat you alive…'

Chapter 11

"You've got to be kidding me!" I cried. Bear stood in the doorway of my new office with a self-satisfied smirk on his face.

"I take it you approve?" he asked.

"Like it? I love it!" I said, twirling around in a delighted circle. The room was massive, almost twice as big as my apartment. It was a corner office and made up completely of windows and steel. A huge bouquet of roses was sitting on the credenza behind my desk. I walked over to it and read the card.

Chloe,
The sky's the limit!
All my love,
~Bear

"Thank you, that's so sweet," I said, smiling over at him. He walked in and led me to the window.

"Look," he said, pointing at the incredible view. "You can see everything from here. There's the Empire State Building. And there's the Old Met Life Tower over there," he whispered, bringing his face close to mine as he pointed them out. I shuddered at the heat rolling off of him. The chemistry between us was flying like sparks and being this close to him was proving very difficult. "That's the Williamsburg Bridge, it's my favorite."

"It's beautiful," I said, leaning over and kissing his cheek.

He pulled away and shook his head.

"Not at work," he said.

"Oh, sorry," I replied. "I forgot."

"That's okay," he smiled. "I'm glad you like the office."

"I do," I said, turning to face him, "but honestly, Bear, don't you think you might want to hire someone more qualified? Someone who's done this before?"

"Nonsense. Like I said last night, I believe in you, Chloe. Have a little more faith in yourself. You'd be surprised what you can accomplish when you set your sights high. That's the only thing separating anyone from success, really—believing that you can do it. Once you have that, and a little bit of courage, you can do anything."

"I want to do a good job for you, that's all," I said.

"Don't worry about making mistakes. We all do. That's why you surround yourself with experts, to keep yourself in check. You can run everything by me before you make any major decisions, if it makes you feel better, but I trust you'll have good judgement."

"You barely know me and you have such faith in me," I said. "Why?"

"I think I know you better than you realize," he shrugged.

I smiled at him gratefully and turned back to the view. I took a deep breath, feeling like I was about to jump off a cliff.

"Alright," I said. "I'll give it a shot!"

"Good girl," he whispered, his eyes trailing down my body, sending shivers of delight through me.

I closed the distance between us and I couldn't resist reaching out and touching his arm. As soon as I did, I realized how much I missed his touch. I vowed to never drink that much wine around him again. He put his hand over mine and squeezed gently, smiling down at me as he nodded encouragingly.

"Everything's going to be okay, Chloe," he said.

"Thank you, Bear," I whispered. "For everything. And for being such a gentleman last night."

He smiled and lowered his voice.

"Don't worry about it," he growled. "I'll take my frustrations out on you later."

I swallowed hard and my stomach flipped. I bit my lip and looked back up at him before pulling my hand away from his.

"I look forward to it," I nodded, as we walked out into the hallway, a perfect picture of employee and employer, nothing more.

"That's what I like to hear," he said. "Now, let's go meet your new assistant. You can look over all the blueprints and figure out what you need. You have a budget of three million dollars. Let me know if you need more."

I froze in place and he kept walking.

"What did you say?" I asked.

"What's wrong?"

"Three million dollars, Bear?" I said, my voice high and squeaky.

"I said you could have more if necessary," he said, with a flippant wave.

"Bear! I've never handled that kind of money before."

"Handle it? You don't handle it, you spend it. It's not that hard, Chloe. Money gets easier to spend the more you have, and it's even easier when it doesn't belong to you. Don't worry about it. You'll probably be begging me for more by the end of the project anyway."

I laughed and shook my head.

"Come on," he whispered, his eyes landing on my lips, "before I make you beg for something else first."

My eyes widened with pleasure and I licked my lips.

"That's my girl," he growled, his voice lowering. "Now, listen. Get your self orientated and go home early today because this afternoon I'm picking you up and we won't be back at work until the day after tomorrow. You can start working after we get back. There's no rush right now."

"Alright," I whispered, silently cheering that I would get another chance to be with him tonight. "I'll go easy on the wine this time."

"Good girl," he chuckled, "let's go." He turned on his heel and walked away.

I smiled and followed him.

I was getting very good at following him.

The view was even better than the one in my office and as I watched him walk down the long, narrow hallway, a secret shiver of pleasure passed through me as I realized just how lucky I was.

Maybe Zoe Rothchild couldn't handle him, but I had every intention of letting Bear eat me alive anytime he wanted.

Chapter 12

My assistant, Abby, was a godsend. I tried to ignore the look of horror in her eyes when I told her I had a fashion degree and that I'd never done interior design before, but she was so knowledgeable and patient, that by the time I left at noon, I felt like this was something that I might actually be able to pull off.

Not alone, of course. But with Abby's help and Bear's input, maybe it wouldn't be so foreign to me after all. I had a good eye for fabric and reading the blueprints wasn't that difficult. I felt a lot better after meeting with her and going over everything, so I went home feeling a whole lot better about my situation.

If I could work and be useful to Bear, then maybe it would make everything else a little easier to endure.

Not that I was 'enduring' anything. God, that word has such a negative connotation, but I didn't know what else to call it. It's not like I'd pursued Bear myself. I hadn't asked for any of it, it had merely been thrust upon me, so to speak. But now that I was smack-dab in the middle of it, I was determined to make the most of it. I was hardly enduring anything, I was a full-fledged, willing participant.

Especially because I had yet to identify one bad thing about it all.

A free apartment in the middle of New York City? Check!

A challenging, handsomely paying position for a top development firm in our nation's greatest city? Check!

A drop-dead sexy hunk of man that made me scream like a woman possessed? Check, check, and check!

I had nothing to complain about, so I didn't.

Sure, I had questions.

I didn't know exactly how in the hell I was going to be able to pull this job off exactly, but I had determination and I figured as long as I added a little perseverance and open-mindedness to the mix, I had a good shot.

And I had questions for Bear. Personal questions that were only now starting to take shape in my mind.

Most of all, I wanted to know why. I wanted to figure out what made him tick, what made him move and talk and lead his life the way he did. I wanted to crawl behind his mask and unveil his secrets. I wanted to know things about him that nobody else knew.

I'd been thinking about Zoe's warning in the bathroom at the restaurant, contemplating whether I should mention our meeting to Bear or not, but so far I'd kept my mouth shut. Telling him seemed so petty. Nothing she'd said made any difference.

Sure, Bear could be a little rough, a little domineering, but so far, he seemed harmless really. He'd certainly not hurt me and he'd had the chance last night.

After he insisted on saying goodbye at my front door, I'd gone straight to bed, peeling my clothes off as I stumbled to my bedroom, cursing myself the whole way for drinking too much wine. I'd spent the entire day working myself up, anticipating fucking Bear again and I'd blown my chance.

I had no idea how long this little game we were playing was going to last. He could end it at anytime. Sure, he'd told me I could, too. He'd insisted on that safe word.

Peaches, of all things! I knew I'd never look at a peach the same way again.

But anyway, that didn't mean he wouldn't just change his mind at any point.

Maybe he didn't have the patience for inexperienced two-drink Chloe going way past her limit. I was pissed at myself because I knew better. And I'd ruined our entire night, even if he'd been a complete and utter gentleman about it. When he'd made me touch his cock to see how hard it was, it only reminded me of what I was missing out on—as if I could forget that beautiful monstrosity between his legs.

So, I'd fallen naked into bed and tried my best to ease my frustrations. Nothing I did worked though, no matter what. I finally feel into a deep, dreamless sleep that only made me more frustrated by the time I awoke.

I was determined not to let any of those events repeat themselves tonight.

It'd been a good day and by the time I returned to my apartment, I was beat. I drew a bath in the huge soaking tub and made a cup of hot tea to relax, determined to leave the wine bottle corked. I was also hoping for a second wind, because I had no idea what to expect tonight. Bear hadn't given me a lot of details, so I had no idea where we were going. He'd said we wouldn't be home till tomorrow, so I packed an overnight bag and laid out a pair of casual black slacks and a red silk blouse on the bed to wear.

I had an hour before he was due to show up and once again, my nerves were raw. He'd been so different each time I'd seen him, and I never knew who was going to show up — the sweet, kind gentleman or the demanding, raunchy sex machine. I was really beginning to like them both but after going to bed so unsatisfied last night, honestly, I was hoping for the latter.

When he finally showed up an hour later, I opened the door with a smile. He was dressed casually tonight in dark jeans and a black sweater. It was the first time I'd seen him in a pair of jeans and the outline of his cock bulging against the denim sent chills up my spine.

"Hello, Beauty," he said, kissing my cheek before walking in.

"Hi, Bear," I replied. "Can I get you something to drink?"

"No, I'm fine," he said, grabbing my hand and pulling it up to press his lips against the back of it. "I'm happy to see you. You look beautiful, as always."

"Thank you," I replied, feeling the dreaded blush rush to my cheeks. "I'll just grab my bag then."

"I should have mentioned that we're going somewhere very cold and very rugged. You might want to repack. You won't need much. Just jeans and sweaters and a warm coat if you have it. We'll be staying in most of the time."

"We're going somewhere colder than here?" I exclaimed. "What's colder than here? The North Pole?"

"Well, it is Christmas time, isn't it? We could give Santa a visit."

"I've always been afraid of Santa," I laughed.

"Really?" he laughed. "Don't worry. We're going North, but not that far. I have a cabin up in the Catskills. Trust me, there will be plenty of warmth. You can park yourself by the fireplace the entire time, if you want. I'll do all the stoking," he winked.

"Sounds heavenly," I replied with a smile, feeling giddy that I was finally going to be alone with him for a while. "Then repacking is definitely in order. I'll be right back." I grabbed my bag and headed back to my bedroom.

Ten minutes later and I was a much happier camper. I'd traded my silk slacks for my favorite pair of Levi's and pulled the Pendleton sweater Marie had gotten me for my birthday last year over my hand. I stuffed my jeans with my favorite pair of worn-out Frey boots and filled my bag with a few more pairs of jeans and some warm socks. I left one pair of black stilettos in my bag and threw in a tiny black dress, just in case we went out somewhere nice.

When I walked back out to Bear, he greeted me with a smile.

"You look much more comfortable," he said.

"I feel much better! Shall we?" I asked.

"Let's go," he said, grabbing my bag from me and opening the front door. A few minutes later and we were in the back of his limo and pulling away from the curb.

"How long is the drive?" I asked.

"We're not driving," he said. "Just wait. You'll see."

"Mr. Mysterious, huh?"

"If that's what you want to call me," he shrugged.

"I can think of a bunch of things to call you," I teased.

He reached over, interlacing his fingers with mine and leaning in close. He kissed me gently and peered into my eyes.

"You can call me anything you want, Beauty," he said, brushing his lips against mine.

"I'm excited to spend some quality time with you," I said.

His laughter caught me off guard.

"Are you? You have no idea what you're in for," he said.

"Oh? Should I be worried?" I asked.

He shook his head. "Not really," he said. "But I did tell you I would take my frustrations out on you later, didn't I?"

"I seem to recall something like that, yes," I replied. Something was changing between us. There was a comfortableness now, a familiarity that wasn't there before. Maybe I was just finally relaxing a little bit, maybe it was because I could finally breathe around him, but for some reason I was now able to look him directly in the eye without the urge to pull away. I was able to flirt with him, talk back to him without stumbling over my words.

"Don't worry, Chloe," he said, his eyes gentle and soft. "I'd never hurt you."

"I never thought you would," I whispered.

"Good," he replied, squeezing my hand. "Oh, look!" he said, pointing out the window. "We're here."

I looked up and squinted my eyes.

"We're at the office," I said.

"There's a lot more to this building than just offices," he said, with a wink. "Let's go in."

He grabbed my bag and helped me out of the limo. He greeted the doorman and the guy at the security desk, slipping them both hundred dollar bills before leading me to the elevator.

"I know I have a lot of work to do but I had no idea you were such a slave driver," I joked.

"We're not going to work!" he teased. He pressed the button for the roof and I looked at him curiously.

"You'll see," he said. I nodded, waiting patiently, drinking in the warmth that was rolling off of him. I sniffed the air, inhaling the musky scent of his cologne. I wanted to etch the scent into my memory. When the doors opened, he led me down a small hallway and another man opened a door at the end of it, greeting Bear as if they'd known each other forever. Bear slipped him a bill, too.

As soon as the door opened, a blast of air hit us forcefully. The loud flapping of propellors was deafening. When I saw the huge, shiny black helicopter waiting on the helipad like an enormous spider, I shook my head.

"A helicopter?" I screamed at Bear over the noise.

"It's faster than a car," he yelled with a shrug, grabbing my hand. "Duck your head!"

We ran towards the helicopter and all I could think about was getting decapitated. I crouched down, probably much more than was required, but I figured I'd rather look like a wobbling duck than a headless woman. Bear jumped in first, then he pulled me up after him. The driver was wearing headphones and waved at us.

"Hey, Alex!" Bear greeted him. Alex was hidden behind enormous headphones and a microphone that went around in front of his mouth. He threw me a wave as if we'd known each other and he wasn't some stranger that was taking my life into his hands, all of a sudden. I looked around. *Should I be signing a waiver or something to get on this thing?*

"Good evening, you two! It's a great evening for a ride! Crystal clear out there tonight!"

"It certainly is! It's good to see you, brother! Thank you!"

"My pleasure, Bear!" he yelled. Bear helped me buckle my seat belt and I sat there shaking in my boots. I'd never been on a helicopter before and all I could think about was every time I'd ever seen one before on television.

They either didn't have doors or someone was jumping out of them, or both. That is, if they weren't crashing into the side of a mountain in a fiery collision of death. I was grateful to see that this one did indeed have doors that were firmly closed by the guy outside. But then I remembered that I wasn't wearing any panties, and my Mother would be horrified if I was found dead without them. I spent a good five seconds contemplating if would be better to be found dead with dirty underwear or no underwear at all.

Bear slipped a pair of headphones over my ears and within seconds, the helicopter rose, shifting slightly to the side and sending my heart plunging straight into my throat. I grabbed Bear's hand as fear spread through my veins.

He patted my hand reassuringly and smiled at me.

"Alex is the best pilot in town. Don't worry, Chloe. Look at the city—it's amazing!"

And indeed it was. The helicopter whisked us up and around the building, weaving through the skyline of Manhattan like a slithering snake, the lights sparkling below us getting smaller and smaller as we rose higher into the star-studded sky.

"You can see the everything up here," I marveled. Bear nodded, his eyes reflecting the lights from the buildings. I squeezed his hand and kissed his cheek. "Thank you for this."

"My pleasure, Beauty, my pleasure," he replied.

The ride lasted for about an hour, the city falling away behind us as we headed north. Soon, the cityscape turned to open fields, the hills covered in lush dark blue forests that bordered perfectly lined crops and from up there, the horizon seemed to stretch endlessly. I found myself wishing it wasn't so dark now that we were out of the city, because I knew there was so much I was missing, but mostly because I couldn't stop thinking about how the darkness increased the chances of the helicopter crashing into a hidden mountain and here I was panty-less.

By the time we started to descend, we were submerged in darkness and I was gripping Bear's hand like a vice. My heart hadn't stopped racing the entire trip and when Bear pointed to a light up above and told me that was his cabin, I finally exhaled with relief that this would be over soon.

Of course, I hadn't even thought about the landing.

It looks so easy and smooth on television, doesn't it? It hovers neatly over a big X on the ground and gently glides back down to the Earth like a graceful crow, right?

Wrong!

If only that were the case in this situation.

Unfortunately, I had no idea about the adventure that was in store for me.

The cabin was nestled high on the edge of a cliff, a log cabin only in the sense that it was made of logs. It was not a cabin. It was a palace, cut from logs. It was lit up from the inside, a warm glow pouring from the windows like a beacon in the night. I scanned the landscape around it, but in the dark I could only see trees surrounding three sides of it and the side that we were approaching faced the edge of a very steep, very tall cliff, with only darkness plunging below it.

"Bear," Alex yelled over his shoulder, as he approached the cabin, "do you need help with the ladder?"

"Nope, I've got it," Bear replied.

"Ladder?" I asked, confusion filling my head. We'd jumped in easily without needing any ladder.

"I'll just hover over the edge, as usual, alright?" Alex called.

"Hover?" I squeaked.

"That's great, Alex," Bear said, before turning to me. "Don't worry. It's only scary the first time."

"What are you talking about?" I asked, my hands beginning to tremble.

"You'll see," he said, as he unbuckled his seat belt and scooted around me. He shuffled around in the corner and pulled out a collapsible ladder and put it next to the door.

"Alex, I'm ready when you are," he said.

"Ready for what?" I cried.

"Coming right up on it," Alex replied. I looked out the window and saw the cabin quickly coming closer. Alex slowed the helicopter down until we were right next to the cliff, the house only yards away.

"I'll drop the bags down first," Bear said, pushing a button. The door opened and I gasped at the force of the air that hit me. He pulled off his ear protection, grabbed my bag and threw it out the door.

"Bear!" I cried, my mouth open in shock. His bag went next and I shook my head, straining to look down for them. I was still buckled in my seat and paralyzed with fear.

"You go first," Bear said, before leaning down and attaching the ladder to some hooks on the edge of the bottom of the helicopter. The ladder fell, cascading down the side of the helicopter and dangling wildly in the air to the ground below.

My head began shaking, my mouth unable to form any words. This was fucking insane. *Go first?* Was he out of his mind? My ass was staying right here in this seat!

"Chloe," Bear said, his voice turning stern and serious. "This only looks dangerous. It's perfectly safe and I do it all the time."

"You're filthy rich, why don't you have somewhere to park this fucking thing?" I screamed.

"Because I would have had to cut down a bunch of old-growth forest to do so and I care about the Earth more than a minor inconvenience like this."

My mouth dropped open in disbelief. *Minor inconvenience?!*

"How is staying alive a minor inconvenience?" I yelled.

"I told you I'd never hurt you," he said, reaching out a hand to me, his dark blue eyes peering into mine deeply. I tried to drink in his courage, his faith in me, his strength. I was certain I didn't have enough on my own to get down that ladder. "You have to go. It's the only way."

"This is fucking nuts!" I yelled.

"I know," he said, shrugging. "Now come on!"

"Goddammit," I muttered, taking a deep breath and unbuckling my seat belt. I grabbed his hand with my shaking fingers and let him lead me to the edge. I looked down and took a step back. It was so far! The ladder was so loose, too—just hanging there flapping in the wind like a loose thread on the edge of a ragged coat.

"I don't think I can do this," I said, bile rising up in the back of my throat.

"Yes, you can," Bear said. "As soon as you get started, the ladder will tighten up with each step you take and the ground is right there below you. It will take ten seconds tops and then your feet will be on solid ground. I'll be right behind you, I promise." He squeezed my hand and I tried again.

Deep breath. Step forward. Don't look down. Try not to puke.

I shook my head and let the chant repeat over and over in my head.

Deep breath. Step forward. Don't look down. Try not to puke.

"Grab my hands and get on your knees, then lower your foot down to the first rung," Bear instructed. I looked at him, sure that his face would be the last one I was ever going to see. Forget dying in a fiery crash on the side of the mountain, I was going to fall into the abyss below.

At least it's him, I thought. If I was never going to see another human face, it might as well be one as stunning as his.

He kissed me and smiled down at me.

"Seriously, don't worry, babe, you'll be fine," he said. "But you need to wear this, just in case."

He held up a harness and a helmet and my eyes widened.

"Jesus, Bear," I said, my first complaint. I couldn't help it. "Do you have something against normal transportation?"

"Helicopters are fast," he shrugged.

"Fast, right," I murmured, as I stepped into the harness that fit around my pelvis and hooked onto the helicopter. The helmet was a little too big and when Bear tightened the chin strap, I felt like a scared little kid being pushed out of the plane by her dad.

I watched as he put his own harness on and fitted his helmet to his head before he motioned to the edge.

"It's go time," he said. "Alex can't hover here forever."

"Right," I replied, sliding my feet to the edge and looking down again.

Deep breath. Step forward. Don't look down. Try not to puke.

The cabin below looked so warm, so damned inviting. Unfortunately, I felt like I had to fight through a pit of snakes or something to get to it. I groaned and sank to my knees. Bear grabbed my hands and I turned around, sliding a foot out into the air. When I lowered it, I felt the rung and pressed down.

"Good girl, that's it," Bear murmured encouragingly. "Keep holding my hands, that's it. Now, put your other foot down."

My body swung loosely, the stability of the helicopter giving way. I screamed, clutching Bear's hands until I couldn't any longer, then putting first one foot, then the other on the rungs and then it was just me and the ladder, swinging in the air.

Deep breath. Step forward. Don't look down. Try not to puke.

"Oh, god!" I yelled, fear ripping through me as I looked up at him.

"Don't stop! Keep moving, Chloe!" Bear demanded from above.

My stomach flipped upside down, the feeling of being weightless and out of control only serving to freak me out even more, my hands and feet frozen on the rungs.

Move Chloe! I silently yelled in my head, forcing myself to move again, first my foot and then my hand. Slowly, I traveled down the ladder, holding on for dear life. My moment of worrying about my panties, or lack thereof, was gone. I was so sure I was going to be torn into a million pieces on my descent to death, none of that would matter.

The air whipped around me and my body swung a little, but not as much as I had imagined it would. I took a few more steps down and when I saw I was only a foot or so away from the Earth, I smiled a little and looked up at Bear. He stared down at me, his handsome face full of confidence in me.

It was just what I needed. I released my grip, falling to the ground in an unceremonious puddle of shaking limbs and trembling lips.

"Yes!" I cried, when I felt the ground below me. I opened my hand, my finger sinking into the cold snow like I'd never felt it before. I turned my head, kissing the ground.

I'd never been so thankful for gravity in my life.

I watched in awe as Bear quickly and effortlessly descended the ladder behind me, easily falling to the ground like a graceful cat, before turning to wave at Alex as he pulled the ladder up behind him.

"See you soon!" Alex cried.

"Thanks, brother! Safe journey home!"

Alex nodded, closed the door and the helicopter took off in seconds, leaving us standing alone in front of Bear's cabin with nothing but our two bags.

"You could have warned me about that," I said, as Bear reached down and pulled me to my feet.

"And miss the look on your face?" he teased, pulling me in for a hug. "No way!"

I let his arms wrap around me, grateful for the return of the simple stability that I took for granted. His warmth was comforting and I melted into him.

"You did good," he said.

"Thanks," I replied, the shaking in my voice muffled by his chest pressed against my face. I was so shaken up and yet I couldn't deny the tiny thrill I felt knowing I'd pulled it off without killing myself.

"Let's go inside," he whispered into my hair. I nodded and he pulled away, swooped the bags up and we trudged through the snow into the cabin.

Chapter 13

I'd never seen a more beautiful place.

"This place is absolutely amazing, but you're sure we couldn't have just driven here?" I asked. Bear sat the bags down by the door.

We walked straight into the great room, the huge vaulted ceilings accented by huge, wooden beams. A huge bear rug lay in front of a massive stone fireplace that reigned over the room, reaching all the way up to the highest point of the ceiling. A huge fire was already roaring in it. The great room opened up to the second floor, with a long cat walk lining the farthest wall, making the second floor look like an open loft. The windows were the biggest I'd ever seen and as I spun around, drinking in the room, I saw nothing but darkness and twinkling stars out of them.

"Do you always repel in like a Navy Seal?" I asked.

His laughter echoed off the walls and I delighted at the way the skin around his eyes wrinkled. Suddenly, all the tension was gone from his face. He was relaxed, happy and calm. The hardness that usually lingered behind his eyes had disappeared.

"It takes about four hours to drive here. With Alex, it takes one hour," he shrugged. "I didn't want to fight traffic and I don't like wasting my time. I have to get back tomorrow night because the day after tomorrow I have an important meeting with one of my contractors. I'd rather spend that time with you, Chloe."

He closed the distance between us, wrapping his arms around me and kissing me deeply. I was already breathless from the unexpected near-death scenario and the intensity of his kiss ripped the rest of the oxygen right from my lungs.

I damn near fainted in his arms.

"Let's get settled," he said, pulling away and looking down at me, his arms firmly secured around my waist. "I'll tell Bruce we're here."

"Bruce?" I asked.

"Bruce takes care of this place for me. He lives here and when I come up, he cooks for me and helps me out with whatever else I need. You'll love him."

"That explains the fire," I said.

"Yes," he replied. "Don't worry, though. You'll hardly know he's here."

I nodded, my breathing starting to return to normal.

"Are we done with adventure time?" I asked. "That was very unexpected."

He laughed again, sending tingles down my spine.

"We've only just begun, darling," he said, sinking his fingers into my hair and pulling my head back. I gasped in surprise, my nipples hardening immediately as his dark blue eyes peered into mine, the flames from the fireplace reflecting in his dark orbs. "There'll be nothing nearly as dangerous as getting off the helicopter, so don't worry, but don't think for a minute the adventures are over." His eyes flashed with lust and I shuddered. "I brought you here for a reason, Beauty. You want to get to know each other? You have questions? Well, Chloe," he whispered, his voice thick with desire. "I have needs. Hopefully, we can get them both answered while we're here."

I was speechless. His fingers pulling my hair felt so deliciously forbidden. It hurt, but god did I love it. I wanted him to pull harder. I wanted his hands on me. Everywhere. I wanted him to touch me firmly, deeply, everywhere he could reach. I wanted everything he had to offer. And then I wanted more. I peered into his eyes, meeting his hungry gaze with my own, a small smile on my face. His lips captured mine in a passionate, fiery kiss and I whimpered, opening my mouth, submitting to his heat, igniting it with my own.

We melted together, his hand sliding from my hair as his arms slid around me, holding me tightly as his tongue tangled with mine and everything around us disappeared. The heat from the fire was no match for the heat that flowed between us.

Heavy footsteps sounded behind us and I jumped away from Bear like I'd been shot.

I'd forgotten where we were and that we weren't alone.

Bear wasn't fazed. He laughed at my reaction and greeted the man who rounded the corner with a huge hug.

"Bruce, it's been too long," he said, patting the large man on the back. He was as big as a linebacker, his wide shoulders stretching the thin fabric of his white t-shirt. He wore jeans and was barefoot. He was handsome, but nowhere near as handsome as Bear. He had long blonde hair and his tanned skin made him look like he lived in the sun. But it was his smile that was his greatest attribute. I liked him right away and his apple green eyes were kind and open.

"You must be Chloe," he said, pulling away from Bear's hug and hugging me close. "It's very nice to meet you."

"You too, Bruce," I replied, as he released me.

"How've the slopes been treating you?" Bear asked.

"Killer, dude! There's some serious pow-pow out there this year. I've been waking up at the crack of dawn for the last week to get a go at the freshie," he said, his blonde waves framing his sun-drenched face.

"You always loved to shred the flake, brother," Bear said. I looked back and forth, completely lost. Pow-pow? Freshie? Flakes?

I made a mental note to ask Bear about it later.

"Excuse me," I said. "I'd like to freshen up. Where's the restroom?"

"Of course! I'll get you something to drink, too, Chloe. Red wine okay?"

I caught Bear's eye and he winked. I wasn't about to fall into the wine trap again.

"I'd love a cup of tea, please."

"You got it," Bruce said. "The loo is down the hall on the right."

"Thank you," I replied, turning away and leaving them to their ski-bum talk. Their voices faded away as they began talking about black diamond trails or something. I knew nothing about skiing. I'd gone once with Harlan and a few friends who were experts at it and they made it seem like it was as easy as riding a bike.

No, it fucking wasn't.

They'd persuaded me to just jump in with both skis, so to speak, and led me to the top of the intermediate slope before I'd even learned to stop or go or even stand up properly. Then, they zipped down the mountain, leaving me there to figure out how to get down all by myself—which consisted of me standing up and falling down over and over until I reached the bottom. By the time I made it down, I swore I'd never do it again.

I spent the rest of the weekend bundled up with a book by the fire in the cabin we'd rented while they skied their expert asses off. I'd been so mad at Harlan after that weekend that I didn't speak to him for a week afterwards.

I walked down the hall, in awe of Bear's cabin. The entire house seemed to be made of wood. Log beams, log paneled walls, and the railings on the huge stairs matched the thick logs that made up the railing that lined the cat walk up top. I felt like I was in the biggest tree house in existence. The amazing thing about it was the coziness, though. In spite of its enormous size, the crackling fire and the soft brown couches and tapestry rugs made it inviting and warm.

By the time I made it back to Bear and Bruce, I never wanted to leave.

Bruce handed me a huge mug of steaming tea and excused himself quickly, leaving Bear and I alone. We stood next to the huge fireplace, the warmth penetrating my skin and warming my bones.

"Feeling a little calmer now, I hope?" he asked.

"I'm fine now, yes, thank you," I replied.

"You have to admit it was a little exciting, right?" he winked.

"If you call nearly dying exciting, sure."

"What is life without risk, Chloe?" he asked.

I opened my mouth and promptly shut it. He had a point. I'd spent my life risking nothing, always taking the safest route when pressed. At least I had until lately. Coming to New York was the first risk I'd taken in a long time and it had already led to some of the most exciting moments of my life.

"I guess you have a point," I admitted.

He leaned down and brushed his lips against mine quickly.

"I'm glad you're starting to see things my way," he replied.

"Do I have a choice?" I asked, laughing.

He grew serious at my words, taking my cup from me and setting it on a table behind him, before turning back to me and pulling me into his arms. I snaked my arms around his waist, reveling in his closeness, inhaling the musky scent of him.

"You always have a choice, Chloe. If you had insisted, I would have made Alex turn the helicopter around and we'd have gone back to the city."

"That's not what I meant—,"

"—that's why I made you create a safe word. I never want you to do anything with me that you don't want to do. In or out of bed." His eyes squinted in concern as he peered down at me.

"I know, Bear," I replied, "I appreciate that."

"Good," he said, kissing me again, "it's important to me."

"I understand," I nodded. Okay, so maybe I didn't fully understand, because I still had so many questions, but I think I was beginning to.

His insistence on clear consent made me respect him immensely, though. Did I feel like I had complete control? Maybe not. But honestly, that was part of the thrill.

Someday, I'd use that safe word, I'd say no, just to test him. But not today. Not now. I wanted nothing more than to say yes to everything when it came to him. He was testing my limits and in turn I was testing them for myself. I had no idea how far we would go, how far I wanted to go, but I knew I'd only figure that out by taking it further and further.

I just wasn't sure what that looked like.

I could only hope he did.

"Bruce made us a lovely dinner. Are you hungry?"

"I'm starved," I replied. And I was.

"Good, you'll need the fuel for later," he growled, as he reached down and squeezed my ass. My nipples hardened under my sweater, anticipation rushing through my veins. "Come on, let's eat."

We walked hand in hand into the dining room, which perfectly matched the rest of the house. A huge slab of redwood with live edges made up the dining table, surrounded by antique shaker chairs.

A feast was laid out for us.

"Bruce did all this? This looks amazing!" I said.

"Bruce is my best friend. He's an amazing cook. I'm an awful cook. He used to be a District Attorney in Manhattan but he burned out after ten years of watching innocent men go to jail. He's equal parts hippie and ski bum. He has a huge heart and that kind of work, while he was doing it with a pure heart, proved to be too much for him. Every case broke his heart. It's impossible to leave that kind of work at the office, you know?"

"Wow, yeah, I can understand that," I replied, as he pulled out my chair for me and I sat down. He sat across from me and poured wine in our glasses from a bottle that Bruce had already opened.

"Not too much," I said, throwing my hand up. "I don't want a repeat of the other night."

"You weren't so bad," he said.

"I was bad enough that you didn't stay," I said.

"Well, as I said then, we have plenty of time," he said.

"Do we?" I asked, slamming my mouth shut as soon as the words flew out.

Bear cocked his head and smiled.

"Don't we?" he asked. "Are you planning on going somewhere any time soon?"

"No, but—to be honest, Bear, I have no idea what is going on here. So therefore, I have no idea how long to expect it to last."

"That's fair," he said. "I haven't exactly been an open book, have I? And this is hardly a typical situation."

"Yeah," I whispered, looking down at my empty plate. Bruce had made pot roast and potatoes and carrots, surrounded by bowls of fruit and big silver platters of cakes and pastries and pies.

"Look, we have also have plenty of time to talk, Chloe. Eat!"

"Okay," I said, piling roast on my plate. We ate silently, stealing glances at each other as we devoured the incredibly delicious food.

"How often do you come out here? If I had Bruce to cook for me everyday, I'd never leave," I said.

"I try to get out here at least once a month, if not more. The city gets to be too much sometimes and I come out here to unwind. I bought the land five years ago and it took a year to build the house. There's also a little cottage out back that Bruce lives in full-time, with a little stream behind that. I'll show you in the morning, it's beautiful."

"This whole place is just stunning, Bear," I replied.

"It's an entirely different world than my penthouse in the city," he said, between bites. "You'll see it soon."

I nodded, once again wondering what I was supposed to think about all of this. Where was this going? Were we dating?

Were we just fucking? He was acting like I was his girlfriend almost and we'd still not defined or clarified what *this* actually was.

"Why did your parents name you Bear?" I asked.

"They didn't," he smiled. "It's actually Barrett. One of my friends at school started calling me Bear in the eight grade. My parents hated it, so I adopted it just to piss them off."

"I see. Tell me about your childhood," I asked.

"Must I?" he winked. I shrugged in response. I had to start somewhere with my questions and the beginning always seemed like a good place to start. "Alright, alright…let's see. Where should I begin? My parents were both overachievers. Mom was a real-estate developer from London. Dad was an investment banker from Queens. They met when Mom came to the States for a conference, but she hated him at first. He chased her all the way back to England and finally won her heart during afternoon tea at the Brown Hotel. Dad had done all his research, finding out the best place to take her in the city. Queen Victoria used to take her tea there every day and Dad regaled Mom with stories of the Royals all afternoon. She said as soon as he began reciting the recipe for the famous orange cake they baked from scratch there at the hotel, she knew she loved him, just for making so much of an effort to impress her."

"That's a sweet story," I said.

"It is. Unfortunately, the rest of the story doesn't tingle the tongue quite as pleasantly."

"No?"

"No. Mom relocated but she basically had to start her career from scratch, which took most of her time. Dad was already a workaholic, so they rarely saw each other. The honeymoon period ended quickly. They were working so hard and spent so little time together that when she found out she was pregnant with me two years later, she didn't believe it. She made the doctor take the test three times. To say I was a surprise is an understatement."

"I see," I replied, so happy to hear about his past finally.

"After I was born, Mom went right back to work and I was raised by a parade of nannies."

"Oh, dear."

"The nannies weren't bad. They were nice enough, I guess. But even though my parents weren't around, they both insisted on ruling my life with an iron fist. Making every decision for me and regulating my activities like their own schedules. I was constantly running from music lessons to Latin lessons to soccer practice. I didn't really get to be much of a kid."

"Did you ask for more free time?"

"I tried. But I knew negotiating with me wasn't something high on their list of priorities, so I gave up after a while. I did what they asked of me, what they thought was best for me, whether I liked it or not. Most of the time, I hated the things they made me do."

"Like what?" I asked.

"Well, let's just say if I never see another trombone in my life, I'll be happy. I hated soccer, too. I wanted to play football and basketball and all the full-contact sports, but Mom insisted she wasn't about to let her only son play such barbaric games."

"What else were you interested in?"

"I wanted to be a writer, actually," he replied. "I loved literature and growing up, I dreamed of being the next Mark Twain, or maybe a poet, but Dad said writers didn't make money these days and insisted I find a more lucrative career."

"I see," I replied. "Do you still write?"

"Not really," he shrugged. "I wrote a few screenplays in college. I have a half-written novel that keeps me up at night sometimes, but I don't really have time for those things these days. My company takes up a lot of my time and energy."

"It's important to find a balance, though, isn't it?"

"I guess that's what people say, but I've never been much of a balanced individual. I tend to go all-in with everything I do."

"I see," I said, feeing a slight blush creep up my neck.

"What else, Chloe?" he asked, smiling at me, his eyes deep as the ocean.

I took a deep breath, the warmth of the wine spreading through me deliciously.

"Where are your parents now?" I asked.

"Dead. Long gone. Dad died of stomach cancer and Mom killed herself a year later."

"Oh, my god!" I exclaimed. "I had no idea."

"It's okay," he replied. "I don't talk about it much. It happened my senior year at Yale. I finished school and started my company right away, determined to make it on my own. Sure, I inherited tons of money and I could have just lived off of that, become a writer and hung out on the slopes with Bruce for the rest of my life, but I needed to be in control of something. They'd ruled my life for so long, once they were gone, I was free. It's hard to explain."

"I think I understand," I replied, softly. "I'm sorry about your parents."

"I'm not," he said. "I'm glad they died. Now, I have a life. Now, I make my own decisions. I do whatever I want, when I want, even if I tend to be a little obsessive about it," he said, his voice lowering to thick, husky growl. "I give the orders now."

I swallowed hard, nodding solemnly as everything suddenly began to make sense.

"Look," he continued. "I know I'm not like everyone else. I'm blessed that I had those two as parents. They taught me a lot about what it takes to succeed in life, they instilled a serious work ethic in me. They left me a ton of money that enabled me to start the company on the scale that I needed to. I wouldn't be who I am without them. But until they were both dead, I had no idea who I was, Chloe. If someone had asked me if I wanted to buy a pair of brown boots or black boots, I would have asked one of my parents first. It wasn't that I didn't have opinions, it's that I didn't trust the opinions I did have. I was constantly seeking their counsel. I think Mom recognized that in that last year after Dad died. She knew it had gone too far. I think she thought she was doing me a favor by taking all those pills and I have to say that she was right."

"Bear, that's…that's…," I stumbled for words, shaking my head.

"It is what it is," he shrugged. "It's the truth. And the truth is always worth speaking."

I nodded, my heart swelling with emotion for him.

"So, now you have this company," I said, wanting him to talk more. I loved the sound of his voice, the deep tones that turned into low growls and murmurs when he turned emotional. I wanted to hear everything he had to say. "And it satisfies you?"

"Does it satisfy me?" he asked, crossing his arms behind his head and leaning back in his chair as he pondered my question. "It allows me the freedom to find satisfaction in other places, I would say. It's definitely work. And sometimes, I get off on it. A big deal goes through in my favor. There's an art to getting your way in business. It's different from personal relationships. You have to be subtle, you have to convince your opponent you're on their side, when you're mostly looking out for your own interests. There's a sense of betrayal to it that I don't enjoy at all."

"No?" I asked, watching the way the muscles twitched in his jaw. Outwardly, he was calm and serene, but the tension in his voice, the way he was gripping his glass, told me a tornado was churning inside of him.

"I don't like betraying people. At heart, I like to think I'm a good person, Chloe," he said, his eyes flashing, searching mine, "you know? I hope you can see that. I have my quirks, but I try to be kind, to do the right thing, to help everyone I can. But, when those deals go through, when I manage to persuade someone to work with me and we create something beautiful together, that is satisfying, yes. I get off on that part of it. So that's why I keep at it. "

"I get it," I smiled.

"I could never have a job where I wasn't the boss," he nodded firmly.

"You always have to be in charge," I whispered.

"Yes. Always," he said. I stared back at him, drowning in his piercing gaze, my body tingling with excitement. There was something so attractive about his unshakable resolve. I'd never been sure of anything in my life. Leading was never something that came naturally to me, and yet I'd envied my friends who did so naturally. Like Marie. Like my Mom.

That wasn't me.

But the steeliness in Bear's eyes every time he nodded like that, his jaw set so firm you couldn't cut it with diamonds—that turned me on. It drew me to him, in a way that I was only beginning to understand myself.

"My life was the complete opposite," I said. "Complete freedom. Matilda was never there."

"Your dad?" he asked.

"Left. I guess Matilda and an infant was too much for him and he hasn't been in my life since I was born," I said. "The glass ceiling has always been Matilda's baby. I admire her for it, I do. But it's hard when you're the only kid at the dance recital without a parent watching. I learned to take care of myself early on," I shrugged. "I didn't need anybody. I was always the one in charge, and I longed for someone to remind me to brush my teeth at night or make me eat broccoli or come to one of my fashion shows."

He nodded at me silently, staring over at me thoughtfully. I'd have given anything to know what he was thinking, to see what he saw when he looked at me. I wanted to know why. Why me? Why was I here? Why had he picked me to spend all this time with?

"Parents have a way of shaping their children in such an insidious way. The subtle ticks we develop, the eccentricities we take on, the very fabric of our souls are woven by how they treat us. It's a sacred act to be a parent. To be able to court that kind of power over another human. It's the ultimate act of oppression, I think. I never want to be that person, the one who could fuck up someone else so profoundly."

"So you don't want children?" I asked.

"Never," he replied, that determination returning to his steely jaw.

"I see," I nodded. "Me, neither."

"You don't want children either?" he exclaimed.

"You sound surprised."

"It's just that most girls your age fantasize about that," he said.

"I'm not most girls," I said, lifting my chin defiantly. I'd defended my stance on children many times before and it was a sore spot with me. Even Marie wanted children someday. She always said as soon as she was done being a slut, she was going to settle down and have a gaggle of kids. The idea sounded exhausting to me.

"No, you aren't are you?" Bear said, reaching over and putting his hand on my knee. He hadn't touched me throughout dinner and the sudden contact shot daggers of electricity up my thigh. My pussy twitched as a shudder began in my neck and traveled down my back. I took a deep breath, struggling to retain my composure. It was merely a slight touch and I was melting. I'd barely had half a glass of wine and I felt dizzy already.

Maybe it wasn't the wine that was shaking me up after all, I thought.

"You're nothing like other women your age," he replied. "Or any other age, I might add."

"I'll take that as a compliment," I said.

"You should," he nodded, reaching over and grabbing the pie from the table. I'd been eyeing it for a few minutes and once I saw Bear cut into it, I squealed with delight when I saw it was peach.

"It's peach!" I exclaimed.

"Yep," he nodded, sliding a slice onto a plate and handing it to me. "Your favorite."

"How did you—oh!" I said, blood rushing to my face. "Right." Of course. The safe word.

Bear's eyes twinkled mischievously as he smiled.

"How could I forget?" he asked.

I nodded, biting my lip.

"I asked Bruce to make it for you," he said.

"Thank you," I said, diving my fork into it. As soon as it landed on my tongue, I moaned in ecstasy. Perfectly sweet and tangy, with light, flaky crust, it melted on my tongue. "It's perfect."

"I told you. Bruce is great," he said. "He'd make a perfect wife," he laughed.

"Is he single?" I asked.

"A perpetual bachelor," he nodded. "He dates around sometimes but as soon as anything starts to get serious, he ends it."

"Kind of like you?" I asked.

"Me? Maybe," he said. "It's a little different in my case. Women don't seem to stick around too long. I've been accused of being high-maintenance and too demanding, if you can believe that."

I laughed, hard, my laughter echoing off the walls. Bear laughed, too, and I felt myself relax even more. I felt comfortable with him. Something about him was beginning to sooth me in places where it ruffled my feathers before, and I didn't know why, but I welcomed it. I wanted to sink into him, in more ways than one. I just wasn't sure how deep it could all go.

I watched him with a smile as he took another bite of pie onto his fork and brought it to my lips. I opened my mouth, meeting his gaze as the fork slid between my lips slowly. I closed my mouth and he slid the fork out, the pie like heaven on my tongue. I swallowed and smiled, licking my lips, the sticky sweetness of the peaches sticking to them.

Bear smiled and then his eyes flashed with hunger.

"Stand up," he whispered, his voice so low I barely heard him.

"What?" I said.

"Stand up. Now." He jaw was set again and his voice was hard and firm. I pushed my chair back, laying my napkin on the table and standing in front of my chair.

"Come here," he said. I took two steps towards him, smiling down at him.

"What are you—," I said.

"Hush. Take off your sweater," he demanded.

"What? Now?" I asked, looking over my shoulder. "What about Bruce?"

"He's in his cabin. He won't come back in here all night," he put one hand on my hip, pulling me closer as he looked up at me. "Take off your sweater."

I shrugged and did as he asked, grasping the bottom and pulling it over my head. I stood in front of him in my jeans and bra, waiting for further instruction. I fought the awkwardness that threatened to overwhelm me and stood stoic in front of him.

He reached up behind me and unfastened my bra, the brush of his fingers sending chills up my back as he slid the bra forward and down my arms, leaving me topless, my breasts heaving with excitement.

He drank me in with his eyes, his gaze devouring my naked breasts before turning back to the table. He plunged his fingers into the pie, scooping the peach filling out with two fingers. I gasped as he turned back to me and smeared the pie filling around my hardened nipples, first one, then the other. I couldn't help but laugh.

"Bear!" I said, watching with amusement as he pinched my nipples with his sticky fingers. He smiled up at me before lowering his head and slowly licking my left nipple. His tongue swirled hotly around it and I shivered with desire. My hands flew up, holding his head, his soft hair falling over my fingers as he licked it all away.

"Bear," I murmured softly, my breath ragged, my body yearning for more of him. He brought his head up, his lips crashing on mine, his kiss hard and searching as he pulled me close, kissing me deeper and deeper until we were scratching at other, the passion igniting between us like a wildfire of lust and need.

He tasted like peaches.

He tasted like me.

He tasted like everything I'd ever known and the only thing I'd ever need again.

I clawed at his arms as he kissed me, needing more of him. Tearing his lips from mine, he knelt down and swooped me up in his arms effortlessly.

"Grab the pie," he growled, dipping me down towards the table.

Chapter 14

I leaned over and picked up the pie from the table, holding it on my chest as he carried me through the house. He trailed down a back hallway and opened a door at the end of it. My eyes widened when I saw it. A small replica of the living room, it had wooden beams lining the ceiling and a huge stone fireplace with another raging fire already lit in it.

But it was the bed that demanded the attention in the room.

Made from logs, the four log posters surrounding it towered over the room, the raw knots and cracks in the wood only adding to the rustic ambiance. Candles were lit on the mantle, a low, amber glow flickering around the room from the fire. Gently, Bear laid me on the bed. I was still topless, my bra and sweater left behind on the floor of the dining room. I knew Bruce would probably find them later, but if Bear didn't care, then neither did I.

As he towered over my half naked body, splayed out on the bed with the mangled pie next to me, I stared up at him hungrily. His eyes flashed with lust as he looked at me, his voice heavy and thick in the darkness.

"Take off your jeans," he growled.

I reached down with a smile, unbuttoning the top button and sliding the zipper down smoothly. I pulled the fabric apart, revealing my bare skin underneath.

"I did what you said," I whispered. "No panties."

"Good girl," he growled. "Off!" he barked.

I jumped into action, pushing the denim over my hips and down my thighs and kicking them off of my feet. He nodded his approval and pulled his sweater over his head, revealing the smooth, perfectly sculpted body that I was quickly becoming addicted to. I bit my lip as he pulled open his Levi's, the distinct pop pop pop of the buttons sending ripples of pleasure down my spine.

When his gorgeous cock came into view, I gasped. It was so perfectly shaped, so hard, so smooth and beautiful that I couldn't help but lick my lips while I watched him grasp it in his hand and squeeze it gently, before kicking out of his jeans. He stood naked in front of me and he paused, staring down at me and shaking his head slowly.

"You're perfect," he whispered. "Do you realize how beautiful you are, Chloe?" He moved between my legs, his body hovering over me as his eyes peered into mine. "Your lips," he said, tracing a finger along my quivering bottom lip. "Your eyes," he whispered, his voice lowering to a rumbling growl, his cock, now pressed against my thigh, throbbing hotly. He pulled his head down, darting his tongue out and licking my bottom lip. "Your taste," he murmured.

He pulled himself back on his knees between my thighs, his gaze raking over my naked body. He reached over and pushed his hand back into the pie, grabbing a handful and smearing it inside my left thigh. He leaned down, kissing my knee, his lips trailing up, leaving feathery kisses on my skin, going up slowly, so slowly, it sent electricity straight to my brain. It took everything I had not to grab his head and push him into my sex, beg him to lick me, plead for him to take me.

Instead, I took a deep breath, silently enduring the torturous pleasure he was raining down on me. Slowly, excruciatingly slowly, his mouth slid up my thigh, licking the pie filling from my skin, his tongue firmly pressing against my flesh until I was whimpering and writhing beneath him.

Once more, he plunged his fingers into the pie, scooping up the sticky peachy sweetness and smearing it higher this time, his fingers sliding up my upper thigh and then lightly moving across my bare pussy, smearing a generous amount on my clit. I gasped at his touch, an electric shock of pleasure ripping right through me.

When his mouth returned, his hot breath searing my skin, my body ignited with yearning for him to fuck me, to lick me, to do something, anything that would provide some relief from the sweet painful yearning I felt.

"Please, Bear," the plea escaped from my lips, despite my resolve to stay quiet. It was impossible. Bear churned up so much emotion, so much turmoil, so much hunger inside of me that I would have burst if I kept it contained any longer.

"Shhh," he said, his lips licking the sweetness from my skin, his mouth inching higher and higher until my hips were flailing towards his mouth. When his lips finally touched my pussy, I thought I would die from the relief, the satisfaction, the pure adrenaline that raced through my veins as I opened my thighs, welcoming him in, pulling him closer, needing all of him inside of all of me.

His mouth worked expertly against me, licking the peaches up quickly and then sliding his tongue along every inch of my quivering pussy, diving deep inside of me, fucking me with his tongue and then siding back up and twirling around my throbbing clit, his mouth pulling pleasure from my body that I'd never felt before.

When his finger slid inside of me, I cried out into the darkness. He pulled my clit into his mouth, sucking rhythmically, sucking hard, his mouth so perfectly skilled that I was sure he'd sold his soul to the devil for that mouth.

His fingers and mouth felt amazing, but they weren't enough. I needed so much more. I needed all of him, every single inch of him as deep as I could get him.

"Bear, please, oh please," I said, his mouth working so perfectly against my clit. "Don't stop, baby, please, don't stop…"

Over and over he sucked my clit, fucking into me harder and harder with his fingers, until my body froze in motion, my orgasm washing over me like a tidal wave of sensation, my body frozen in pain, frozen in pleasure, suspended in time in a second of release until I crashed back down, my entire body tingling with the pure joy of being alive, of being a woman, of being so blessed that I was here, now, with this beautiful man.

My arms snaked around him, pulling him close as he rose up, his mouth capturing mine in a frenzied kiss of peaches and pussy. I melted below him, my entire body turning to a puddle of pleasure and softness.

And he allowed me that.

For about thirty seconds.

I clung to him, my breath slowing, my senses returning slowly. He kissed me, over and over, his sensual, slow kisses quickly turning hard and rough again, until he pulled away, his eyes flashing down at me.

Hunger. Lust. Savage, animalistic need.

That's all I saw. The gentleman was gone. The man that had taken me in the restaurant had replaced him. The hard set of his jaw only made him sexier and the darkness in his eyes sent my heart racing with excitement.

"It's my turn," he growled, before grabbing my waist and flipping me over. I laid below him, not sure what he wanted me to do.

"Get on all fours," he said. I slid my knees under me, raising up my ass and looking over my shoulder back at him.

He was incredible. Hard, strong, determined, and deliciously naked—everything about him was a masterpiece of masculinity that I wanted to study, memorize, engrave onto the darkest, deepest parts of my soul.

I didn't realize it then, but that's exactly what was happening.

Chapter 15

In one smooth, velvety rush of pleasure, his cock sank deep inside my quivering pussy.

I rocked back towards him, determined to experience every single inch of his delicious hardness. Deeper and deeper, he inched forward until a savage growl escaped from him, his throbbing hotness piercing the deepest parts of me.

"Yesssss," I moaned, waves of pleasure lighting up every inch of my flesh with shivering, tingling electricity. I pushed back against him, lowering my shoulders to the bed and raising my ass higher, opening myself up to him like a wanton hussy. I didn't care. I didn't even think about it. Offering myself to him so brazenly, so boldly, seemed like the most natural thing in the world.

His fingers dug into the tender flesh of my hips as he grasped me roughly, pulling back onto his cock as he began pounding into me with the force of a bull. I gasped, surprised at the roughness as he slammed into me harder and harder. I sank down into the bed, bracing myself with my knees as he sped up.

I gasped as he slapped my ass, my head flying around and looking at him. He was lost, his gaze trained on my ass, at his cock sliding between my lips. He hit me again, harder this time, and I whimpered as I felt the heat rush to my ass cheek, as he continued to pound into my pussy relentlessly. Over and over, he slammed into me, hitting my ass between thrusts, alternating sides as he began moaning loudly, his cock swelling side of me.

I turned back around, melting into the bed, relishing in the intensity of so many different sensations. His cock deliciously sliding into me contrasted against the faint pain of his pounding hips, the fiery burning of the blows against my skin, all mixed together until I was lost completely, my mind falling under his spell, my body submitting to it all, welcoming every inch of pain and pleasure that he inflicted.

He reached down, grabbing a fistful of hair at the nape of my neck, pulling my head from the bed, forcing me to arch my back as he pulled me back to him. He pulled my head to the side, capturing my lips in his, his tongue delving deeply into my mouth as his cock slammed hard into me, over and over, his fingers tightening with every thrust until I was whimpering into his kiss. He softened his grip, his fingers sliding out of my hair as his hands found my hips again as he held on tightly and began pounding into my pussy faster and faster, my juices flowing over his hot, throbbing shaft.

"Fuck me, Bear, harder, harder," I encouraged. He was pounding into me so hard that my vision had blurred, all awareness of anything outside of his punishing hammering faded away and all I could do was search for the magical release that my body was crying out for. He hit my ass again, his blows raining hard and fast, my skin burning beneath his touch.

Abruptly, he pulled out and I whimpered in protest, my pussy crying out for his hardness. He grabbed my hips, turning me around swiftly. I fell back on the bed, my thighs falling open as he smoothly slid back inside, his lips finding mine as I snaked my arms around him, my hands clawing at his taut flesh, his muscles rippling under my fingertips.

He kissed me deeply, his cock thrusting inside of me sensuously, his tongue twirling around mine, our bodies searching for the deepest part of the magic together, our hips dancing as one, rhythmically seeking the only thing in the world that mattered in the still darkness of the night.

We found it. Frantically crashing over the edge together, his cock exploding with a forceful heat that shot right through me, his fiery release sending me crying and writhing below him, seized by the pleasure that rushed over me, my body shuddering and shaking and clutching onto him in a desperate attempt to keep from floating away into the air.

I clung to him, never wanting to leave, never wanting this moment to end, never wanting whatever this was to change into anything else.

I'd never come this close to perfection, to heaven, to ecstasy.

In that moment, he was life.

Chapter 16

I thought he was done. I thought we'd drift off into a blissful sleep, dreaming of rainbows and unicorns and everlasting love.

It had been that magical.

After a few moments of allowing me to lay my head on his chest, my fingers lazily running through the soft hair on his chest, my entire body left in a daze, he shifted. I moaned a soft protest as he slid out from under me and off the bed.

"Come back," I pleaded, as I watched him walk across the room to a large armoire in the corner. His ass was a picture of perfection, flexing deliciously with each step. He opened the doors and pulled something out, turning back around and heading back. I gasped when I saw his cock was rock-hard again, throbbing and huge, like the last hour hadn't even happened. Hunger flashed in his eyes like a thunderstorm. "What are you doing?" I asked.

"I'm not done with you," he growled. I couldn't help but smile.

My eyes trailed down to his hands and my heart skipped a beat when I saw what he was holding. Long, black silk scarves dangled from his fingers.

"What are those?" I asked.

"You ask a lot of questions," he replied, his voice tense and low. I shivered, my entire body waking up again, tingling with excitement and anticipation.

"I told you I had questions," I teased, a slow smile spreading across my face.

"I'm not in the mood for questions," he growled, crawling onto the bed towards me, his dark eyes smoldering.

"What are you in the mood for?" I purred, running my hands over the curves of my breasts and down my hips like a preening peacock displaying its feathers. He turned me on like nothing I'd felt before.

For once in my life, I felt wanted.

I felt sexy.

I felt alive.

His mouth crashed into mine, his tongue forcing its way in, his kiss deep and urgent and searching. I whimpered, arching my back, pressing my breasts into his bare chest. He tore his mouth away, the storm in his eyes raging.

"I'm in the mood to fuck you again," he growled. "Harder this time."

I shuddered at his words. He'd damn near fucked me into the next universe already and I didn't know how much harder he could get without killing me. I nodded, slowly, opening my thighs and sliding my hand down to my clit, my fingers pressing into it, circling it, over and over, before sliding a finger inside of my soaked pussy, in and out, in and out.

"Fuck me harder, Bear," I whispered. "Fuck me as hard as you can. Fuck me all night."

He groaned, swallowing hard, the heat rolling off of him like an inferno of animalistic need. Quickly, he set to work. He grabbed my hands, spreading them over my head, tying them easily as he secured each one to the posts above my head.

"Bear, you don't—," I began to protest.

"—Hush. This is what I want."

I bit my lip, watching him as he pulled my ankles down, securing them with the ropes just as he had with my hands. Soft and silky, the satiny black fabric rubbed against my wrists and ankles sensuously. I tried to pull out of them, but they were knotted tightly and I couldn't move but a few inches in either direction.

Bear stood up, inspecting his work, his cock bobbing between his legs like a baseball bat. My eyes were glued to it, my mouth watering, my pussy quivering as I yearned for him to slam himself back inside of me.

My eyes widened as he reached down, his fingers wrapping around his shaft, his fist sliding up and down his cock, his face taken over by the savagery of his urges.

Gone was the refined businessman.

Gone was the charming gentleman.

Gone was the teasing playboy.

The Bear standing in front of me was pure man, pure animal, pure passion.

He climbed back up on the bed, his hands running up my thighs, his fingers digging into my pussy, finding my clit and circling it lightly, sending jolts of delicious pleasure shooting to my center, my head falling back on the bed as I cried out. His fingers slid inside of me, one, then two, then three, and I gasped at the fullness. I was so wet, so ready, I welcomed all of him. He pulled his fingers out, pointing them all together and sliding his entire hand inside of me, hooking his fingers as he came out then shoving them back inside, fucking me over and over with his fist until I was squirming and crying out, my orgasm quick and sudden.

"I'm coming," I screamed, as he continued pumping his fist inside of my spasming pussy until I was thrashing around below him, my body on fire as my juices flowed over his hand. He pulled out slowly and I gasped for breath, my breasts heaving, my nipples hard as rocks.

"Good girl," he said, leaning down, his mouth landing on my pussy, licking up my juices as I moaned in pleasure, my hand sinking down into his hair, pushing his head harder against me. I'd just come, I felt like I'd died from pleasure and his mouth just kept it going, his tongue lapping up every drop of my juices, darting inside of me, his tongue fucking into me and sliding up to my clit, until I was coming again and again, my body seized by a symphony of shivers and shudders and waves of deep emotion that left me gasping for air.

"Good girl," he growled again as I felt him lift his head up. I opened my eyes to find him hovering over me, his blue eyes almost black with desire as he slid his cock into me again. I opened myself up to him, every inch of him like a revelation of life.

I struggled against my restraints, hating that I couldn't wrap my entire body around him like I so desperately craved. He fucked into me so hard, slamming into me so powerfully, shoving my body further and further up the bed with each thrust.

He reached up, grabbing a fistful of my hair, pulling my head back as he drilled into me.

"You're my little slut, aren't you, Chloe?" he growled. My mouth gaped open at his words and I froze. He squeezed my hair harder, pulling my head back a little, his eyes flashing.

"Say it," he growled. "Tell me you're my little slut, Chloe," he demanded.

I nodded, my pussy spasming around him, his words shooting right to my pussy.

"I said, say it!" he yelled, his fingers tightening even more around my hair as he slammed hard into my pussy. I gasped in pain, crying out.

"Yes, Bear, yes—I'm your slut!"

"Mmm," he groaned, his cock swelling inside of me. "Good girl."

Over and over, his cock hammered into me, my pussy wet and swollen and hot, his cock sliding into me like a machine as he kissed me hard, pulling away again before I could kiss him back.

"Say it again, don't stop," he insisted, reaching down and pinching my nipple hard. I gasped in pain again, jolts of searing heat shooting through me. "Tell me what I want to hear, you little slut."

Something snapped in me. A shedding of inhibitions, a shrugging off of all traces of decorum, I lost a part of me in that moment that I'd been holding on to all of my life. I let go and it all floated away, there was no more self-judgement, no more preconceived notions of who I was supposed to be or how I was supposed to behave. Everything fell away and I became a different version of myself, a sexier version, a wilder version.

I'd found freedom in those restraints.

I didn't care about anything but completely losing the person I used to be and becoming whoever I was in Bear's arms, in Bear's eyes.

"Yes, fuck me, Bear!" I yelled, my voice louder than ever before. "I'm your slut, my pussy is all yours, please just fuck me, please don't stop, please don't ever stop fucking your pussy. It's all yours. I'm all yours. Please just take me!" It didn't even sound like my voice. It was husky and low and full of yearning and lust.

Bear's eyes told me everything I needed to know. They shone with approval and flashed with the stormy lust that I craved to unleash in him. He was everything I wanted in that moment, the only thing I needed.

With abandon and uninhibited power, he fucked me with the force of a thousand gods, using my tied down body for his every pleasure, coming inside of me over and over and over, until we lay spent and exhausted in each other's arms hours later, the sunlight breaking through the darkness of the night sky, throwing embers of golden light over our naked flesh as morning dawned a new day.

Chapter 17

We slept till noon, the smell of eggs and bacon waking us up.

Bear stirred beside me, pulled my naked body close to his and slipped his hard, throbbing cock inside of me from behind. Sleepily, he thrust inside of me, his arms snaked around my waist, spooning me as he fucked me slowly. I moaned, arching back towards him, loving the softness of his fucking compared to last night.

He'd fucked me so hard and for so long, that my pussy was raw and sore, but even still, the soft gentleness of his thrusts was so sweet, it was like a salve on my sensitive skin. His hardness sliced into me, filling me up deliciously as he shifted on top of me. I wrapped myself around him, my thighs, my arms, my lips finding his as he fucked me faster and faster until he was coming inside me again, his entire body stiffening under my fingertips, his muscles rippling as he filled my pussy with his heat as I spasmed around him.

Slowly, he slid out of me, kissing me gently and staring into my eyes.

"Good morning, beautiful," he whispered.

"Good morning," I said with a smile. He looked so handsome in the morning, his hair tousled around his head. Everything we'd done last night raced through my head. I felt so close to him now. He was still a bit of a mystery, there were still so many things I didn't know, or didn't understand about him, but the little bit I had learned seemed to explain so much.

I hadn't had time to wrap my head around it all yet, but seeing him here now, the morning sunlight shining on his naked flesh, his beautiful blue eyes bright and clear as they shone down on me—somehow it was all starting to make sense.

"Smells like Bruce made us breakfast," he said, tracing a finger around my nipple. "Are you hungry?"

My stomach growled in response and we burst out laughing.

"Let's get up," he said. "There's somewhere I want to take you today."

"Do we need a helicopter to get there?" I asked.

"No," he laughed, kissing my nose. "Not unless you're a very bad girl," he growled.

"I can be whatever you want me to be," I replied, lifting my chin daringly. Just being in his arms made me feel sexy. I'd never have said anything like that with Harlan, or anyone else for that matter. He made me so much more daring than I'd ever been before.

His eyes widened at my words and a slow, sexy grin spread across his face.

"Now that's what I like to hear," he brushed a kiss across my lips and stood up, reaching out a hand and pulling to my feet. We stood at the side of bed and he reached down, grabbing a handful of my ass and pulling me into his body.

"Don't forget what you said last night," he said, his voice a low, sexy warning.

"That I'm your slut?" I whispered, pressing my tits into him.

He squeezed my ass harder and I moaned, pressing harder into him.

He groaned, his cock twitching in my hand.

"Or, that my pussy is yours?" I cooed, standing up on my tiptoes and licking his bottom lip daringly. "Which one?"

"If you keep that shit up, I'm going to have to bury my cock inside of you again," he growled.

"Would that be so bad?" I asked.

"Never. But I need fuel, woman. Food!" he squeezed my ass playfully again and pressed his lips against my nose. "Don't worry, I'll fuck you again real soon, baby."

"I hope that's a promise," I whispered, smiling up at him.

"If I were you, I'd take it more as a threat," he winked. "I don't plan on being very gentle."

"If you haven't figured it out by now, Bear, I like it hard," I replied.

His laughter echoed off the walls, my heart soaring with happiness.

"I could tell," he winked again, grabbing my hand and pulling me towards the bathroom. "Shower. Get dressed. Let's have breakfast. We've got all day to fuck. I need to talk to Bruce for a bit. Meet you in the kitchen."

"If you say so," I said, pouting.

"Good girl," he growled, slapping me on the ass as I walked away.

* * *

By the time I'd showered and dressed and made it back to the kitchen, Bruce was gone.

"What happened to Bruce?" I asked. Bear was sitting at the table, surrounded by a huge spread of fruit and juice and pastries and omelets.

"He had to hit the slopes before it gets too late. He's addicted to the powder, that guy," he said.

"You two seem very close," I said, sitting down and grabbing a croissant.

"We are," he said. "He's my closest confidant. Probably my only confidant, actually."

"You don't get too close to people?" I asked.

"Not usually," he said. "It takes a lot of work."

"That's true," I said. "It's good that you have at least one friend, I think. I couldn't live without my friend Marie."

"Does she live in Portland?"

"Yes."

"Tell me about her."

"Hmm," I said, between bites. "Marie is the exact opposite of me. She's vivacious and vibrant. A real firecracker, some would say. She's bold and extravagant and always says exactly what is on her mind. You'd love her."

"Is that why you're drawn to her? Because she's not like you?"

"Yeah, I think so. She was a really good friend to me when we met in middle school. I needed a girl like her in my life, someone to help bring me out of my shell a little."

"I understand," he said.

"So where are we going today?" I asked.

"The old Catskill Mountain House site."

"What's that?"

"It's beautiful. It used to be the site of a grand hotel that was frequented by New York's elite in the late nineteenth and early twentieth centuries. It has sweeping views of the Hudson Valley. I thought we'd do a little sight seeing."

"Sounds good," I nodded, staring across the table at him. He looked so good in the morning light, so healthy, so fresh, so vibrant. And he looked calm and quiet and kind. The storm that was brewing in those eyes last night was gone and he stared back at me with the gentleness of a puppy.

Now that the intoxicating effects of flesh-on-flesh had faded, I was left to deal with the churning in my heart. I could feel myself beginning to have feelings for him, real feelings, feelings that I had no clue how to deal with. This was all fun and games, sure, but it didn't necessarily mean that this was love.

But, dammit, if he kept smiling at me like that, then these feelings were definitely going to be something I had to reckon with. And I had no idea if that was something that I was experiencing all by myself or if he felt it too.

For all I knew, I was just a good time to him.

But maybe that was okay, too. I was certainly having a good time myself and I didn't want that to end anytime soon.

That's why I kept my mouth shut and my questions to myself. I didn't want to overwhelm him with probing questions that maybe neither one of us was ready for yet. Maybe it was best to let things unfold slowly. Maybe it was best not to force anything.

I made a silent vow to myself to just let go and enjoy myself and do my best not to overthink the situation, which I was usually prone to do.

"How far away is this hotel?" I asked.

"It's not there anymore, actually. Burned to the ground in the sixties. But it's not far. Only a few minutes by helicopter, actually."

"Shut up!" I said, laughing. "You said no more helicopters."

"No I didn't!" he said. "Never say never, Chloe. You never know when a helicopter might come in handy!"

"What a life you lead," I teased.

"It has its perks, that's for sure," he replied. "But no worries, darling, your chariot is waiting in the garage."

"Now that sounds more like it!" I quipped.

His laughter was light and easy and it lit up his eyes, the darkness fading into a joyful song that seemed to radiate from him. This man had so many layers and I was finding it completely delightful peeling them back. There was the serious businessman, the loyal friend, the generous employer, the courageous adventurer, the smoldering lover and the demanding fuck machine, and now, here in front of me at the moment, the relaxed, happy, laid-back all-American man.

So far, I'd enjoyed seeing them all. We finished breakfast in silence and he led me to the back door of the house. Now that the sun was out, I could see that his property stretched far behind the main house that was located on the edge of the cliff we'd rappelled onto last night. A beautiful stream snaked behind Bruce's tiny, modest cottage, and huge snow-covered, old growth trees towered over the entire property like a thousand snowy guards.

"This area reminds me of Oregon," I said. "So many trees…"

"Yes, it's a lot like the Pacific Northwest, only colder. We have many of the same trees you do—fir, birch, beech, pine, lots and lots of oak."

"I love it, Bear," I said, as we walked around his property. "It's absolutely beautiful."

"I'm glad you love it," he said, reflections of the trees shining in his eyes. The snow crunched beneath our feet as we walked hand in hand back to the house. "You're going to love the view of the Hudson Valley from where we're going."

"I can't wait," I said.

A black Jeep with huge tires that would rival the biggest dualie's in Eastern Oregon was parked in his garage.

"This thing is a beast," I remarked.

"Isn't it?" he said, his voice bursting with pride. "This thing is one of my most prized possessions."

"It is?" I asked.

"Hell, yeah. I can go anywhere at all with it. It practically drives on water, that's how amazing it is."

"Please tell me we aren't driving through water today," I said.

"Come on, Chloe, where's your sense of adventure?" he teased.

"I have one. I just don't think it's quite as wild as yours."

"Well, baby steps, right?" he winked, as he slid behind the wheel. I jumped in beside him and he roared out of the garage like a rocket. I held on to the door handle, my heart racing as I remembered the fear I'd felt jumping out of the helicopter last night. I wasn't sure my heart could handle too much more of Bear's escapades.

After winding through his property, we were on a regular road within minutes. I reminded myself to breath and pried my fingers from around the door handle. He looked over, sensing my nervousness and laughed.

"Don't worry, darling. Nothing too adventurous or dangerous today, I promise," he said. "Relax. Enjoy yourself."

"I'm definitely enjoying myself," I smiled. "I'm working on the relaxing part."

"Good girl," he said, reaching over and patting my knee. Every single time he called me that it sent a shock through my system. I think he knew it, too. I think he knew exactly what he did to me. How could he not? I was such a hot mess of lust and desire, I could barely breathe around him.

After about ten minutes of driving down winding forested roads, Bear turned into a half-empty parking lot.

"There's a bit of a hike, but it's worth it," he said, cutting off the engine.

We jumped out of the Jeep and he led me down a trail to the right of the lot. We passed some small shrubs and a bunch of large rocks, but it wasn't really anything spectacular. But once we rounded a corner and exited the trail, it was like the entire world opened up before us. The sweeping view was absolutely stunning, the valley below us expanding for what seemed like forever.

"My goodness!" I exclaimed.

"I know! It's incredible, isn't it?" he said. "This is the site of the old hotel. It's gone now, as I mentioned earlier, but the view will never be gone. I love coming here."

"I can see why," I said, drinking everything in. A few other people walked around also, but the cold and snow seemed to be a natural people repellant.

He grabbed my hand and led me to the edge of the cliff and we stared down below at the mesmerizing view. The cliffs and hills and trees were all lined with snow, the landscape of the valley below rising and falling like the curves of a woman. A light fog hung heavy in the distance, casting an eerie feeling over the entire valley.

"The escarpment trail lines the entire valley," he pointed to the edge of the mountains in the distance. "It's probably my favorite hiking trail in the entire state of New York."

"It's beautiful, Bear," I said, turning to him. "Thank you for bringing me here."

"Let's walk for a while," he said, grabbing my hand in his and leading me to the trailhead. The view was spectacular and seemed to change with each step we took. His hand was warm in mine and my heart swelled with emotion at the beauty of the Earth.

"I never want to leave this place," I whispered to him. Birds chirped over our heads and the sun shone through the trees every now and then as it peeked out from between the clouds. It was incredibly cold, but the warmth of his hand and the heat rolling off of him as I leaned into his side kept the shivers at bay.

"Well, it's not going anywhere. You can come back here as often as you want."

"It definitely reminds me of home," I said.

"Do you miss it? Home?"

I paused, contemplating his question before answering. Truth was, I hadn't really had time to miss anything. Everything had been such a whirlwind since I'd arrived, and honestly I hadn't really thought about much at all except Bear.

"No," I finally answered. "At least not yet."

He nodded, smiling at me quietly. We walked for a while, leaving the people wandering at the cliff's edge behind us until we were alone on the trail. Our words fell away as we took in the majestic view below as we wandered along, the peacefulness of the wilderness washing over us. My heart slowed, my breathing steadied and the stillness of the forest seemed to seep inside me, capturing all the restlessness and anxiety and dissolving it until nothing was left inside of me but pure serenity.

We rounded a corner and the view changed, the valley below us twisting and turning. After a while, we came upon a huge house-sized boulder that jetted out at an angle over the cliff, the trail winding around behind it. We stopped to admire the view. I stood there in awe, mesmerized. Bear stood behind me and slipped his arms around my waist, leaning in and brushing a kiss against my neck. I moaned, arching back into his warmth.

"You look so beautiful out here in the wilderness," he murmured.

I smiled, loving the solidness of him behind me.

"Thank you," I said. "I've always been amazed to think that people used to live out here, surviving in such harsh conditions, barely shielded from the elements."

"Yes, we've gotten soft as humans, haven't we?"

"I suppose," I replied.

We stood there for a moment, looking down into the valley, Bear holding me close. After a moment, his grip on me tightened and I felt his cock stirring against my ass. He let out a low groan and I couldn't help but smile.

"Chloe," he growled, "you make my cock hard as a rock every time I'm near you."

"Hmm," I murmured. "Am I supposed to apologize for that?"

He laughed and turned me around, kissing me hard before replying.

"No apologies necessary," he growled. I looked up into his eyes and saw the rawness there. I swallowed hard, my heart racing as I stared up at him. "But you do need to take care of it."

"Here?" I asked in surprise. "Now?"

"On your knees," he ordered.

"But the snow…" I said, looking back down the trail. "The people…"

"Then just squat down and don't worry about the people! Do as I say!" he barked, unzipping his jeans and pulling out his beautiful hard cock. I jumped into action, bending my knees and gripping his shaft, sliding it between my lips, his guttural moan my reward.

My nipples hardened as I twirled my tongue around the velvety skin of the head of his cock, sucking his hardness into my mouth. I couldn't help but keep my eyes open, the fear of getting caught rushing through me as I frantically slid his cock in and out of my mouth. His hips moved, his hands holding my head tightly as he fucked his cock into my mouth, his hardness throbbing against my tongue deliciously.

"Stop!" he demanded and I jumped again, looking up to him. He reached for my hand, pulling me up and walking me over to the huge boulder we were behind and pressing me up against it. I faced the rock and he stood behind me. I looked over my shoulder, waiting for instructions.

Surely, he's not going to fuck me right here, I thought.

I was so wrong.

He reached around me, unfastening my jeans and pulling them down around my thighs, exposing my bare ass to the freezing cold. I gasped as the frigid wind hit my skin.

"Bear," I protested. "It's so cold…"

"Not for long," he said, smacking my ass with his warm palm, hard. It stung, sending shivers of pain and pleasure through me. He hit me five more times and by the time he was done, my ass was warm and tingling.

His fingers sank into my hair as he grabbed it and pulled back, whispering in my ear.

"I don't like it when you complain," he growled, before shoving his cock into my pussy fast and hard. I whimpered at his words, at his sudden thrust inside, but quickly, I submitted to him, opening myself up to him, lifting my ass as much as I could to allow him easier access to my pussy.

He moved against me, the force of his blows pressing me into the boulder as he fucked me harder and harder. His cock felt amazing and my ass was still stinging from the blows of his hand, the cold air blowing against the hot, red skin sending shivers throughout my body. The faint sound of approaching voices startled me and I turned my head, my eyes wild with fear.

A slow smile spread across his face as he whispered in my ear, his cock thrusting hard and fast inside of my quivering pussy.

"Are you afraid, Chloe? Are you afraid someone's going to see what a nasty little slut you are? Are you afraid they'll see your bare little pussy getting pounded by my hard cock? Are you afraid they'll see who you really are?"

His words shot daggers of pleasure straight through me, my pussy spasming around his cock as I cried out.

"Bear, fuck me, please Bear!" my voice echoed through the canyon below.

The voices became louder and closer as he slammed into me, harder and harder, until he was coming too, his cock bursting inside of me as an animalistic growl escaped from him.

I shuddered, not from the cold, not from the fear of getting caught, but of the sheer strength of his thrusts and his orgasm ripping through me.

Slowly, he pulled out, slapped my ass a few more times and then took a step back. I looked over my shoulder at him, my hands up against the rock as I looked back at him, waiting for further instructions as the voices came closer.

He smiled, a slow, sexy smile spreading across his face as he nodded.

"You can get dressed," he laughed, zipping up his pants.

I leaned down, pulling up my jeans and fastening them, just as the group of people rounded the corner. My face flushed hotter than my ass as we walked past them and back down the trail. Bear grabbed my hand and laughed.

"My name sounded pretty good echoing through the valley like that," he teased.

I shook my head, laughing, the thrill of the moment still running through my veins.

Chapter 18

The drive back to the city was stunning. The winding roads were lined with towering snow dusted pine trees with a stream flowing beside us almost the entire trip. Ribbons of pink sunbeams broke through the trees as the sun sank into the horizon, casting shadows across the blankets of snow that covered the ground —it was an enchanting winter wonderland and I never wanted to leave.

"It'll be dark by the time we get back to the city," Bear said. His hand rested on my knee and besides the few moments behind the rock, he'd been the perfect gentleman all day. He was quiet and calm, a little reserved even. I was starting to see that was his usual demeanor until his cock got hard, and then apparently, all bets were off.

It was a little hard to get used to, but I was trying. He flipped on a dime today and I had no idea that was coming. The old me never would have fallen to her knees like that. Outdoors? In public? When I heard those voices approaching, I almost had a heart attack.

He's definitely keeping me on my toes, I thought.

I squirmed in my seat, my pussy still sensitive and swollen from the poundings he'd been giving me the past two days.

"I had a wonderful time," I told him, as I gazed up at the sky, capturing the moment in my mind, drinking in every single detail. "Thank you for bringing me here."

"I'm glad," he said, glancing over to me with a smile. "I told you the helicopter ride would be worth it."

"It wasn't the ride that was so bad," I laughed. "It was leaving the helicopter behind."

"Goodbyes are never pleasant, are they?" he teased.

I laughed at his joke, shaking my head.

"Can I ask you a question?" I said.

"Oh, yes, the questions. We didn't quite get to them, did we? Sorry about that."

"We managed a few," I replied.

"But not enough," he said.

"I can't imagine I'll ever be finished asking questions," I laughed.

"Good point," he said. "I'll remember that. So, we have a little less than an hour left on our drive. Ask away."

I nodded, growing serious as I contemplated how to word what I wanted to know. It was simple, really.

"Why me?" I asked, my voice soft and shy suddenly. "Why is this all happening?"

He nodded, staring straight ahead at the road. For a moment, I wasn't sure he heard me at all.

"Do you remember the first time we met?" he finally asked.

"Yes. At the restaurant, how could I forget?"

"No, before that, years before that."

"Oh, right. At the company Christmas party. I'd just turned eighteen and Mom dragged me with her for the some reason. She'd always been so against me going. I never understood why she made me go that year."

"I told her to bring you," he said quietly.

"You did? Why?" I asked, my head spinning towards him. He looked straight ahead, his steely blue eyes hidden in the flashing shadows of dusk.

"I saw your picture on her desk one day," he continued, his voice low and far-away. "Something about you made me stop and look twice. You were sitting in a crowd of people, at a party or something. Everyone was smiling and talking behind you, but you sat off to the side, with a book in your lap. You'd looked up at the photographer, and it was obvious you'd been interrupted. There was this ethereal light in your eyes, in that flash of a second. It was if you'd been captured—half in the real world and half out of it, as if you were lost in whatever book you were reading and suspended between worlds. Something about it charmed me. I asked Matilda about you."

"Oh, I see," I replied, thoughtfully. I wasn't sure if that was weird or not.

"Matilda's face lights up like a Christmas tree when she talks about you, Chloe," he said. "She's very proud of you."

"Really? That's surprising."

"Is it? She loves you, it's obvious."

"Well, like I mentioned before, she's basically been too distracted by her career my whole life to pay much attention to anything I've done."

"She loves you," he nodded firmly. "Anyway, I asked her to bring you to the party because I was curious what Matilda's daughter would be like in person."

"And? What was I like?"

"You were nothing like Matilda!" he said, roaring with laughter. "You were shy and quiet and withdrawn."

"You asked me to dance," I said, remembering the night clearly. He'd intimidated me. I was still a teenager and he'd seemed so much older and sophisticated than me. And he was so incredibly handsome. He was so far out of my league, I never once imagined we'd be here today. When he'd asked me to dance, I was mortified, but I'd said yes because I didn't want to upset my mom.

"That's right, I did. You remember?"

"Of course, I remember," I said. "It wasn't that long ago." I'd never danced with a man before—only a few boys during high school dances amongst a bunch of other kids our age. It was always awkward and weird and we all avoided the slow dances as much as possible.

Dancing with a handsome man I barely knew at a luxurious grown-up party wasn't something I was prepared for. In fact, I remember being so irritated that Mom made me go, that I put a book in my purse, expecting to sit in the corner by myself and read all night. I'd done just that until Bear had walked up out of the blue and asked me to dance.

"Do you remember the song?"

"Some slow Motown thing," I said.

"It was '*Oh, No*' by the Commodores," he said.

"I can't believe you remember that," I said, looking over at him. "I just remember thinking the lyrics seemed overly sappy and romantic."

He laughed loudly, making me laugh with him.

"I guess they were," he said. "I didn't think about that too much then. To me, you didn't seem like a child, Chloe. You were already eighteen, right?"

"I was," I said. "But barely. What does this have to do with my question?"

"I've been thinking about you ever since then, Chloe," he said, growing serious again.

"You have?" I asked, my voice raising in bewilderment.

"It started when I saw your picture. Then, when I met you, something about you captured me. It was like a switch went off. Like I'd finally found something I didn't realize I was looking for."

"Seriously?" I asked.

"Yes. I know it doesn't make sense," he said, "and you were way too young, too shy, too quiet. You were about to start college, I knew you had so much ahead of you."

"I don't really know what to say," I replied, my mind spinning.

"There's nothing to say. I'm just answering your question. When I saw you again that day at lunch in Portland with Matilda, the feelings I'd had before were only reinforced. But when you so passionately dug your heels in about moving to New York, I saw something else in you that I hadn't seen before. A spark. A quiet determination and yet there was so much more. You seemed lost and wild, like maybe you were looking for someone to guide you. I acted solely on my intuition. I took a huge chance that day. You could have run out of that room screaming. It would have been a huge embarrassment for me. But something else happened, didn't it?"

"Yes," I answered quietly, remembering, "it did."

"Something magical, if you ask me," he replied, squeezing my knee. I looked over at him, a million more questions in my head. I nodded in agreement, quiet again and lost in my own thoughts.

What had he seen in me at eighteen? I had no idea who I was back then. Was I wild and lost? Maybe I was. But isn't every eighteen year old wild and lost?

The thought that I'd been on his mind all this time had completely taken me aback. How was that even possible? I had no idea I was even on his radar. Everything had seemed so spontaneous and random. To think that it wasn't—well, I just didn't know what to think about that.

"I'm sure this comes as a surprise to you," he said.

"That's putting it mildly," I said. We were close to home now, the city sparkling like a blanket of stars stretching out in front of us.

"What did you think of me that night?" he asked. "You were polite enough and danced with me, but I could tell you couldn't wait to get away."

I nodded quietly, remembering, his words putting me right back there in the moment. Mostly, I remembered his hands.

They're so hot! I thought. Mr. Dalton's hands radiated a heat like nothing I'd felt before.

One of his hands was holding mine and the other one was pressed against the small of my back and somehow created the distinct sensation of making the fabric of my dress melt away. It felt like skin on skin, just like the skin of his palm that was touching my palm as we moved together on the dance floor.

He was leading. I'd stepped on his foot twice already, once the left, lightly, then the right, so hard that he'd winced, the skin beside his eyes wrinkling up in deep crow's feet. I could only manage a very quick glance, because his dark blue eyes seemed to be trying to pierce right through me and it was making me nervous.

From the way his hands felt against me and the way he was looking at me, I felt like I was having that dream again that I used to have. You know the one—where you're giving a presentation in class and you look down and suddenly you're naked and everyone's laughing and pointing at your private bits.

It was like that.

Only, Mr. Dalton wasn't laughing or pointing.

He was looking at me the way I looked at that frog in biology my Freshman year in high school. I was so curious back then—I wanted to know everything about it, see every single intestine and ligament and organ. I focused on it like a laser, drinking in every detail.

I couldn't look at him, but I could feel his gaze on my face. My eyes stayed averted and I looked everywhere but at him. I just wanted the dance to be over. Why in the

*world would a man like him want to dance
with a girl like me?*

*He was enormous—not just his body,
but his presence was overwhelming, too.
Way too much for eighteen year-old me to
even begin to have the skills to process.*

*I mean, he was incredibly handsome,
built like a god, don't get me wrong. But
with every word he said, the low rumble of
his voice seemed to vibrate directly to my
gut. I didn't really hear a word, I was so
focused on getting away from him.*

*He was like a flame that I was being
made to touch against my will.*

"Chloe?" he asked, pulling me back to
the moment. "Do you remember?"

"Yes," I replied. "I was just very
overwhelmed by you, that's all I really
remember."

"I got that impression," he said. "That
was unfortunate. But understandable. You
were young."

"I'm still pretty young," I shrugged.

"That's true, but there's a big difference
between eighteen and twenty-six."

"I suppose," I said, my mind trying to
process all of this information. I'd barely
given him a second thought since that dance.
To think that it meant more to him was
bewildering. And a little unbelievable.

He was rich and powerful. He could
have any woman he wants, why would he

waste two seconds thinking of a naive, inexperienced, shy girl he barely knew?

"I imagine this makes you look at me a little differently?" he asked.

"I—well, I don't know. I don't think so. I just don't understand why you'd be interested in a girl like me—now or then."

"You underestimate yourself, you know that, Chloe?" he said, the lights from the city now flashing on his face. "You're a beautiful, intelligent, thoughtful woman. Any man would be lucky to spend time with you. Even me."

I nodded and tried to smile.

I tried to believe him.

I wanted to believe him.

But it all seemed so far-fetched. There wasn't anything all that special about me. To think he saw something in me that I didn't see myself made me question everything.

Who was I?

Have you ever wished you could see yourself as others see you?

I sighed, sinking back into the seat as Bear kept driving, his Jeep immersing us deeper and deeper into the city as he drove me home. Our reflection flashed in the glass windows of the buildings and I saw us—a seemingly normal couple doing a seemingly normal act of driving down a street—and yet, I felt like I was watching a movie, as if none of this was really happening to me.

Believing that I'd catch the attention of a man like Bear, have an opportunity to live in a city like this, to experience the things I'd experienced in the last few weeks, did not come easy or natural. It was far from ordinary, far from normal.

And yet, although I'd been plopped into this life out of nowhere, Bear seemed to act like it was the most natural thing in the world. And now I knew why. He'd been thinking about me for years. He'd played out the scenarios we'd been acting out in his head for years.

But this wasn't a movie.

This was real life.

My life.

And most of all, I needed it to make sense.

I wasn't sure how to make that happen. Maybe I'd have to keep asking questions until something clicked. Maybe I'd get there with the passing of time.

In the meantime, I'd just have to keep pinching myself to remind myself how real it all was.

Bear pulled up in front of my building and turned off the engine. He turned to me, a smile on his face as he pulled me in for a kiss. His lips were warm and soft and so inviting. My body stirred, a deep yearning that never seemed to be extinguished.

"Aren't you coming up?" I asked, between kisses.

"Nope, not tonight," he replied, leaning down and kissing my neck. I shivered, a light moan escaping from my lips. "I have an early meeting in the morning, remember?"

"Right," I replied. "I'll be in early tomorrow, too."

"No, take the day off," he said, shaking his head. "Recuperate. There's plenty of time to get the project done."

He kissed me again, harder this time, my entire body tingling with excitement. I opened my mouth, kissing him deeper, suddenly hating the fact that we were about to be separated. I was growing quite fond of his hand in mine and the thought of going up to my apartment alone wasn't appealing at all.

He kissed me back, hard, the passion growing between us. I moaned, reaching up and touching his cheek, relishing the feel of the stubble he'd grown the last few days under my palm.

We both jumped apart when my phone started ringing.

I yelped, digging through my purse as I searched for it. I found it at the bottom.

"Fuck!" I yelled when I saw Harlan's ugly face on the screen. Punching the top button, I turned it off, looking back at Bear apologetically. "Sorry about that interruption."

"That was your ex calling?" he asked, his eyes flashing with irritation.

"I guess so," I shrugged.

"Does he call often?" he asked.

"What? I don't know…maybe, I guess. I never answer because he's the last person I want to talk to."

"Then why is he calling?" he demanded.

"I—I don't know," I stuttered, taken aback at his tone of voice. He'd changed so quickly. "It doesn't matter," I shrugged. "He's a loser."

"You should tell him to stop calling," he said, flashing me a tight smile.

"That would mean I'd have to talk to him," I said, reaching over and kissing his cheek. I opened the door and grabbed my bag from between my legs and turned back to him. "I had an amazing time. Please tell me we can go back there soon?"

"You bet," he said, his smile widening and his eyes relaxing. I hated seeing him all uptight over Harlan, but he was a man and a very alpha one at that.

"Good!" I smiled back. "I'll talk to you tomorrow."

"Goodnight, Beauty," he called, before I closed the door.

I walked into the building hating Harlan for ruining my moment. As soon as I got in the elevator, I pulled out my phone and blocked his number.

Chapter 19

"So, tell me everything!" Marie's voice boomed into my ear as soon as I picked up the phone. I'd texted her before I'd left to go to Bear's cabin letting her know I'd be out of touch for a few days.

"It was like visiting the North pole but without Santa," I said, as I poured myself a cup of coffee. I'd only been awake a few moments before she was blowing up my phone. "It was very snowy and cold and beautiful."

"That sounds lovely, what else?"

"We went there in a helicopter!" I said. "I had to repel out of it, Marie! His cabin is perched high up on a cliff and there's nowhere up there for it to land."

"Are you sure you aren't dating Jack Bauer?" she asked.

"No," I laughed. "It was terrifying, actually. The rest of the trip was absolutely lovely, though."

"Did you fuck him again?" she asked.

"That's basically all we did," I replied. "Inside. Outside. On a trail overlooking the Hudson Valley in the snow."

"That's amazing," she said. "He must be amazing in bed."

"He's, well—like I told you before, he's a little rough."

"Not too rough, I hope?"

"Rough enough that I have a safe word."

"Oh," she replied, "that's interesting."

"He's interesting," I said. "There's many layers to this guy."

"Well, be careful," she said. "Don't let him go too far."

"It's not like that," I said. "He'd never hurt me."

"Well, don't be so sure. He sounds like he like's extreme sports, repelling out of fucking helicopters and shit!"

"You may have a point," I said, laughing. "He definitely has a penchant for adventures."

"And perversions, apparently," she teased. "How's your butt?"

"My butt?" I asked.

"Last time we talked you had a Princess Barbie plug stuck up your butt, remember?"

"Oh, right. Yes, I'm pleased to report my butt is healthy and happy."

I smiled, sipping my coffee, grateful for my friend. I don't know what I'd do if I didn't have anyone to talk to about all of this.

"What are you doing today?" she asked.

"Having dinner with Matilda tonight," I said.

"How is she taking your new relationship?" she asked.

"She doesn't know," I said. "So keep your mouth shut, you hear me? No Facebook posts or anything!"

"Oh, a secret fling with your Mom's boss, I love it! It's so titillating!"

"It is not!" I asked. "It's just—oh fuck, I don't know what it is. It's exciting. And very new. No need to tell Matilda anything, as far as I'm concerned."

"Well, be careful, you know how psychic she is with you," she warned. Marie had seen Mom's psychic connection with me in person several times.

"I know, I know," I replied. "I have my guard up. I'll be fine."

"Famous last words," she teased.

"Shut up!" I yelled. "Look, I gotta go. I just woke up and I need breakfast."

"Alright, alright," she said. "Call me later—oh wait!"

"What?"

"I forgot why I called!" she said. "Harlan is going nuts looking for you, girl. He's called all your friends now and I guess he called your Mom's old office and they told him she moved, at least that's what he told my friend Jessica. He's been talking about you non-stop to anyone who will listen, insisting he's going to get you back, that he's finally gotten his shit together."

"Oh, please!" I said, rolling my eyes. "What is his problem? We've been broken up for six months, why can't he just let it go?"

"I guess you're just that good," Marie teased. "And apparently Harlan isn't the only one who thinks so. Maybe you should just tell him you've got a new boyfriend?"

"No, way. It's none of his business and the last thing I want to do is talk to that asshole."

"Okay, it's your business. I just wanted to let you know he's been snooping around."

"Thanks," I said. "My plan is to ignore him until he goes away."

"Got it," she said. "Okay, then. That's all. Toot-a-loo!"

The phone went dead and I shook my head as I laid it on the kitchen counter.

Harlan could drop dead for all I cared. I had no intention of ever talking to him again and the fact that I never had to see him again made me happy.

New York was starting to feel really good.

* * *

Max dropped me off at the Italian restaurant near Mom's building before she arrived. After getting us a table and ordering a bottle of wine, I watched the people stream by outside, the snow lightly falling around them as they hustled through the streets. Everyone was bundled up with scarves and hats and thick coats, doing their best to protect themselves from the frigid temperatures.

Oregon winters were cold, but outside of maybe one or two days of snow, Portland didn't get much snow. Lots of rain, sure, we were used to that. But cold like this? Even the worst of our winters couldn't touch this.

When Mom walked in, she was shivering.

"I'd kill for a nice Oregon mist right now," she said as she slid into the booth across from me.

"This cold goes right through your bones!" I exclaimed, pouring her a glass of wine.

"I can't believe people leave their homes in this mess," she said, laughing.

"I know, right? The entire city of Portland shuts down with half an inch of snow. Can you imagine how they'd react to this much and for this long?"

"Seriously, it's been snowing since we arrived. I hope you've been bundling up."

"I have," I replied. "You know what a wimp I can be about the cold."

"Well, if you need to go shopping for warmer clothes, just let me know and I'll give you my credit card."

"I'm good," I said, feeling a flash of guilt for not telling her about Bear. She was being so nice. "I have some savings and I brought a bunch of warm things with me, too."

"Is that a new dress?" she asked, eyeing the red frock I'd bought the other day.

"It is, do you like it?" I asked, neglecting to mention that I'd bought it with Bear's credit card.

"I do," she said. "It's very East Coast."

"Thanks," I replied, smiling at her.

"It's good to see you, Chloe," she said. "Sorry I've been so busy. I knew things would be crazy at first."

"It's okay, I've been busy too."

"So, what have you been up to?"

Ugh, I thought, t*he dreaded inquisition.*

I'd been preparing for this. At least now I had an actual job to report, outside of all the '*dick-tation'* I'd been taking from Bear.

"Well, I saw my office and met my assistant," I said, lifting my chin proudly.

"Excellent!" she said, "I haven't had a chance to talk to Bear in a few days. He went upstate to his cabin. Tell me about the job."

"He's put me in charge of designing the interior of his new hotel."

She froze, her glass raised midway to her lips. She stared at me across the top of the glass, her eyes wide.

"You're kidding!" she said, shaking her head. "That's a three million dollar job. I just saw the budgets for next year yesterday."

"I know, he told me."

"But Chloe—that's absurd. You have no experience with something like that. You don't have a clue what you're doing. Surely, you told him that."

I stared open mouthed across the table at her. I mean, yeah, I had thought the same things, but she didn't have to be so fucking harsh about it. Tiny twinges of anger surged through me and I fought to take a breath. The last thing I wanted to do was make a scene in this tiny restaurant.

"Sure I did," I said, flippantly. "But apparently he believes I can do it."

"I'll talk to him," she said, with a wave.

"No!" I yelled, my voice bursting through the room. A hot blush crept up my neck and I took another deep breath. "There's nothing to talk about," I said, lowering my voice. "I can handle this, Mom. It's not really any of your business anyway."

"None of my business?" she asked. "I beg to differ, Chloe."

"You know what I mean!" I said. "I can take care of this. I can do this job. I don't need you meddling in this opportunity before I even get started."

"Why haven't you gotten started?" she asked.

"What?"

"What have you been doing the last few days?" she asked. "You said you saw your office and met your assistant, but that takes about five minutes. I haven't heard from you in days."

"I've been studying," I said, nodding firmly. I had that response ready ahead of time. "I went to the library and checked out some books on interior design just to get some ideas." Another lie, but I did plan on doing that right away.

"Well," she said, taking another sip of wine. "I suppose it's worth a shot. But that's a huge budget, so don't fuck it up, Chloe."

The anger that was trickling through me earlier had now broken free and was raging through my veins. She didn't believe in me. It was clear as day. And that fact hurt, but I was used to it. I guess I just wasn't used to it on this scale.

Yeah, three million dollars was a lot and this was a huge job, but I had plenty of time to plan and learn what I needed to know. The building wasn't even finished yet. It wouldn't be finished for another year. And if Mom knew the budget for it, then she knew that, too.

But still. It was me we were talking about.

I couldn't help but notice the stark difference between what Bear believed I could do and what she believed I could do.

A slow, fake smile spread across her face and she reached over, putting her hand on mine.

"I'm sure it'll be fine," she said. "I didn't mean to come off so harsh."

"It's fine," I said, pulling my hand away, just as the waiter came up.

We ordered quickly—fettucine for me and manicotti for her—and she launched into a big long recap of the board of directors meeting she'd attended. I only half-listened and she kept topping off her wine glass until the story began to repeat itself. I shook my head, suppressing a laugh. Neither of us could handle our liquor, I guess.

I tried to shake off my anger at her through the rest of dinner. We ate in silence, the soft Italian opera flowing through the speakers and the low din of voices filling in for conversation.

It was after the tiramisu that she brought up the job again. At this point, I was done with her. I couldn't wait to get home to my warm bed and snuggle up with a movie and the chocolate bar that was waiting for me on my kitchen counter.

"So what is he paying you?" she asked.

I blinked slowly, trying to choose my words carefully. Bear and I hadn't talked salary at all, really.

"I'm not sure yet," I said, recalling Bear's words exactly. "He said I would have a handsome salary and full benefits."

"He used those words?" she asked, raising an eyebrow. "What is this, the fifties?"

"Well, if you're the CFO then maybe you should know already," I said, trying to get in a little jab. She'd certainly gotten in enough of her own.

"I looked, actually. And there was no record of a job for you or a salary," she said, her voice steely.

"Oh," I shrugged. "I don't know what to say."

"Well, I'm sure if Bear told you he was going to take care of you then he will."

"Right," I said, unsure how to respond. Bear was certainly taking care of me, but not in the way that she meant.

I'd never been more grateful to see the check brought to the table. I grabbed it quickly and threw my credit card in the folder.

"My treat," I said, trying to force a smile. "Since I'm employed now and all."

"How nice," she said, nodding. "Thank you."

"My pleasure, Mom," I said, already eyeing the door before I'd even put my coat back on.

* * *

Max was still waiting for me, much to my pleasure. It was even colder now and the warmth of the backseat of the limo was like heaven to my shivering body. I'd said the quickest goodbye to Mom ever. She only had half a block to walk home and I was happy to have the isolation of the car now.

It was never easy with her. I knew this and yet every time I forgot, letting myself getting disappointed and hurt with some crazy unfounded expectation that things would be different. I should know better by now.

I sank back into the heated seats gratefully as I watched the city outside the windows. Everyone was so damned busy. Going somewhere fast.

I could sit in the back of this limo and watch them all for hours, I thought.

We were almost to my building when Max took a right on a street he normally took a left on.

I pushed the button and watched as the window between us rolled down.

"Max, I think you're going the wrong way?" I asked.

"I'm sorry, ma'am, I thought you knew."

"Knew what?" I asked.

"Mr. Dalton asked me to bring you to his penthouse."

"Oh," I said, my heart skipping a beat. "I see. That's fine, Max, thank you."

I leaned forward, pressing the button and waiting for the window to roll all the way up before I exhaled. I still didn't know if Max could see me back here with the window up or not, but just having the illusion helped.

I sank back into the seat, a tiny shiver of secret pleasure running through me as I bit my bottom lip. I wasn't expecting to see Bear tonight. The fact that he had summoned me like a damned Mafia boss kind of turned me on, actually. My stomach fluttered with anticipation. I'd not been to his penthouse in the city before, so I had no idea where we were going.

When we pulled up to the building, I gasped. It was the building I'd seen in a million photos of the New York skyline. Two huge towers reached up to the sky, the old architecture of the building was just stunning.

"What is this place?"

"The San Remo? You've never heard of it?" Max said, as he helped me out. We stood on the sidewalk together, staring up at it as the snow fell around us. It wasn't as tall as a lot of buildings in the city, but it was majestic and regal. "Lots of celebrities live here. Mr. Dalton bought the penthouse from Demi Moore last year."

"I see," I said, my eyes huge with awe as I took in the beauty of the building.

"I'll walk you to the elevator," he said. We walked in past the doorman, passing through a gold trimmed door.

"Mr. Dalton is on the 26th floor of the South Tower here," Max said, as we approached the elevator. "I'll be just a phone call away, if you need me, ma'am. Have a wonderful night."

"Thank you, Max," I said, stepping onto the elevator. There was a man in a formal uniform standing in the corner.

"Mr. Dalton's penthouse, ma'am?" he asked.

"Yes, please," I replied. He pushed a button, but just as the doors started to close, someone rushed in. The man pushed his arm out and held the door open for a beautiful grey-haired woman.

"Good evening, Ms. Keaton," he said, greeting her. I looked at the woman and my mouth fell open. Diane Keaton was on the elevator with me! I was star-struck and I had to force myself to close my mouth and not look at her.

"Hello, Johnny!" she said. "Thanks for holding the door open."

"Of course, ma'am," he replied. They fell silent and the elevator rose to the penthouse, dropping her off halfway up. I was smiling ear to ear as she left. But I was also proud of myself for staying quiet and not turning into a gushing fangirl as the poor woman was just trying to get home to her apartment. I'd probably kick myself for not getting her autograph later, but for now, I felt good about my decision.

A sharp ding indicated we were at the top of the tower and I thanked the elevator guy and stepped into a tiny lobby with a door on the side. I took a deep breath and knocked, doing my best not to feel completely out of place in such luxurious surroundings.

When Bear opened the door, all my worries melted away.

His smile was like a beacon in the night and he pulled me into his arms, kissing me deeply and passionately, as if it was the most important thing in the world to do.

Chapter 20

His kisses left me breathless. He didn't take his lips off of mine as he pulled me into his apartment and kicked the front door closed. He pushed me up against a wall, without a word, without a sound, his hands everywhere all at once, pushing off my coat and letting it fall to the floor.

Within seconds, he pulled my dress over my head, leaving me standing there in my bra, panties, stockings and shoes. When he saw my panties, he growled, his eyes meeting mine in an angry flash.

"I didn't think I was going to see you—," I began to explain.

"Stop!" he demanded, reaching down and pulling them over my stockings quickly and ripping them off of me. He threw them behind him as he sank to his knees, his mouth engulfing my bare pussy in an instant.

I whimpered, my knees weakening as his tongue lapped at my already flowing juices. His tongue dove deep, sliding past my outer lips and sinking into me, his hands pulling my thighs apart so he could go deeper.

In and out, it darted out of my pussy, then going lower and sensuously sliding over my ass, my body shivering with forbidden delight. I cried out, his name sliding over my tongue like it was the only word I knew.

"Bear, Bear, Bear…," I cried, over and over, opening my thighs to give him access to the deepest parts of me. My eyes rolled back in my head as the most delicious pleasure washed over me in rapturous waves, my entire soul submitting to him. He lapped between my legs, his mouth hot and wet and expertly drawing every ounce of energy and stiffness from me, until I melted to the ground with him, my bare ass hitting the cold hard marble floor with him on top of me.

He pushed his jeans to the side, hurriedly pulling his cock out and sliding it deep inside of me before I could even touch him. I wrapped my thighs around his hips, my feet resting on his loose jeans. I pushed them down over his ass, exposing his tight, muscular ass.

My hands wandered as he fucked me, my fingers searching for something to grip onto as he pounded into me harder and harder. I wrapped my arms around him, his face next to mine as he groaned and slammed into me, over and over, his cock so hard, so sinfully delicious that I couldn't get enough of it.

"Don't stop," I pleaded, "please don't ever stop."

He growled and kissed my neck, his teeth nipping at my flesh and then sucking, sending shivers of electricity through me. He pulled himself up, his eyes peering into mine demandingly.

"Who are you?" he growled.

"Yours," I whispered, meeting his smoldering gaze, "your good girl, your slut, your pussy…"

His hips slammed into me with each word, hard and rough, each thrust pressing my ass harder into the cold marble below us.

"Good girl," he groaned, his cock throbbing hotly inside of me as he exploded, his hot cum searing the walls of my pussy.

Chapter 21

When I opened my eyes, it was pitch black. Bear's breathing beside me was the only sound in the room. I untangled myself from his arms, doing my best not to wake him.

My skin was still tingling from his touch. Every single time we had sex, he seemed to get a little rougher. At first, I thought he was just into ordering me around, but the more comfortable he became, as more time wore on, he spanked my ass a little harder, or pulled my hair just a little more.

Tonight, he'd handled me like a rag-doll, almost.

He fucked me in just about every spot possible in his bedroom, carrying me in there after devouring me in the foyer. I'd only gotten a glimpse of the penthouse, but what I'd seen was spectacular. His bedroom was huge and my ass knew it better than I did, at this point.

He'd barely said a word to me all night. But he'd kept me talking, fucking me until I was spewing dirty words like a sailor.

As I walked out of his room and closed the door behind me, I could feel the aftereffects of his roughness with each step. Naked, I walked past the huge great room with double windows making up the entire side of the apartment, leading out to a terrace that wrapped around the top of the historic building.

I was dying of thirst and I found the kitchen on the other side of the house.

After finding a glass in a cabinet, I poured myself a glass of water and drank it all, gulping it down as fast as I could and then filling it up again. He'd worked me over so hard this time, and it had felt amazing, but he was testing my limits like they'd never been tested.

I wandered around the apartment, admiring the minimalistic style of the place. It was the exact opposite of his rustic cabin in the woods. It was all smooth lines and sharp corners and empty spaces, with stark sculptures on display in the corners. I padded down a hallway I'd not seen earlier, taking in the abstract paintings that lined the walls.

All the doors of the rooms along this hallway were open, showing off the dramatic views of the city from each bedroom. I kept walking, peeking in each room and thinking about the job I had to do. I knew absolutely nothing about interior design, but whoever designed this place sure did. I tried to remember every detail to use later for inspiration.

I stopped when I came upon a closed door. Contemplating whether or not I should open it didn't last long. I turned the door knob and was greeted by darkness. I felt around for a light switch and flipped it.

My eyes almost popped out of my head when I saw the room.

"What the fuck is this?" I whispered. It took me quite a while to figure it out. The entire room was painted a deep crimson and two of the walls were lined with mirrors. The furnishings were like something out of a movie. Low slung black leather couches lined one wall and a long, sleek chaise sat in a corner. In the middle of the room was a huge contraption shaped like an X with handcuffs hanging from each corner. Hanging from the red walls and grouped together was an assortment of heavy chains, followed by ropes of all sizes and a bunch of different types of whips.

I gasped when I saw those, reaching out and letting my fingers run through the straps of soft leather.

"It's a fucking dungeon," I whispered to myself, my heart racing, my head spinning. I knew Bear was into things that weren't quite normal, but I didn't expect *this*. This was like a professional studio you'd find in some wild BDSM porn or something.

Is this what he was into?

Is this where he'd been leading me all along?

"What have I gotten myself into?" I said, my voice shaking.

"Chloe," Bear's voice boomed from behind me and I nearly jumped out of my skin. "What are you doing in here?"

Chapter 22

"Bear!" I exclaimed. "I was just getting a drink of water." I held up my water glass, realizing how surprised I was that I hadn't dropped it yet at the same time.

"The kitchen's back there," he pointed behind him and I searched his eyes, trying to see what he was thinking. The darkness of the room prevented me from getting a good look at his eyes. I put one foot in front of the other, breathlessly closing the distance between us.

"I know," I whispered, finally standing in front of him. "I'm sorry, I shouldn't have come in here."

"That's right, you shouldn't have," he said. "I wasn't planning on showing you this just yet."

"I'm sorry, Bear," I said, hanging my head. "Let's just pretend I didn't see anything." I moved to walk around him and he reached out a hand, grabbing my arm. I froze, looking into his eyes, searching the dark storm that was beginning to churn in them.

"It's too late for that," he said. "I don't play pretend."

"Okay, well," I replied, my voice quivering. I don't know why I was so nervous, but something in his voice, in his eyes, was unnerving. "We don't have to talk about it. Whatever you want, Bear."

"That's not how this works," he growled.

"Wh-what do you mean?" I asked, looking down at his hand as he gripped my arm tighter

"You have to be punished, Chloe," he whispered. He was naked, too and his cock was hard as rock, throbbing between his legs.

"Punished?" I asked, my voice high with excitement. I didn't know if I should be turned on or go rushing from the apartment. Adrenaline rushed through my veins as I lifted my chin defiantly.

"I didn't do anything wrong," I said. "I don't need to be punished."

His eyes smoldered, his pupils dilating as he breathed heavily, his hot breath searing my lips as he came within millimeters of my mouth. A slow smile spread across his face and he shook his head.

"I think you've forgotten where you are, Beauty," he reached up, grabbing a fistful of my hair and roughly pulling it back. "You've forgotten who you're talking to, haven't you?"

I gasped, the pain ripping through my skull and sending shocks of pleasure straight to my clit.

"How will you punish me?" I asked, my eyes wide, as a slow trickle of desire began rushing through me. If he wanted to play this game, well I could play, too. I was a little intimidated by the whips hanging on the wall but I was trying not to think about them.

"However I damned well please," he growled, his eyes flashing with anger. "I didn't tell you that you could leave the bed, did I?"

I shook my head, biting my lip as I waited for whatever he was going to do to me.

"No, I didn't. The first thing I'm going to do is restrain you, so you don't take it upon yourself to go wherever you please."

I nodded, his fingers still tangled in my hair. He let go slowly, then grabbed my arm and pulled me across the room.

"Move!" he yelled.

I jumped into motion, walking along with him as he brought me over to the huge contraption in the middle of the room. I stood in front of it, desperately trying to meet his eyes. I needed something, some sort of reassurance that Bear was still in there, that he hadn't been replaced with someone—something—else.

He must have sensed it.

He took a deep breath then looked me square in the eye.

"What's your safe word?" he asked, his voice a deep guttural growl.

"Peaches," I whispered.

"Good girl," he said. "You probably weren't expecting all of this. But now that we're here, it's good that you've seen it. Now you can see me for who I really am, Chloe," he nodded slowly, gesturing to the scene around us. "This is me. Take me or leave me. This is your chance to walk away, right now." He motioned towards the door. "You can leave right now, you can leave anytime. It's always your choice, you need to know that and understand that. It's up to you to decide what to do."

I let his words sink in, and his eyes seemed to pierce so deeply into my soul that I felt it. It was like he'd crawled inside of me and he wasn't even touching me any more. His hands had fallen to his sides and I yearned for him to touch my skin, but it was as if he'd found a way to look into the darkest corners of my heart and mind, turning over rocks and lighting up the secrets that I'd kept from myself.

Slowly, I lifted my arm in the air, holding it next to the leather cuff behind me.

"I'm staying," I whispered.

He nodded solemnly, a glimmer of light appearing in his eyes before fading away into the savage darkness that overcame him. It was fast and sudden, too fast, too sudden. His hands fastened the cuff on my raised hand, then the other. My ankles were next, the cuffs tight against my skin. Suspended and restrained, I watched as he stood back to inspect his work.

His stormy eyes raked across my naked body as he nodded slowly.

"You're fucking beautiful," he said. "I knew you would be." My hair hung in waves around my face and I stared back at him. He was so present, so fucking intense and for the first time I felt a surge of fear. There was something so savage about him right now, even more than before, like a predator toying with his prey.

He grabbed something from the wall behind me and I braced myself for the pain of the blow, but instead a wispy softness floated over my skin and I looked down to see a handful of soft leather straps hanging loose around my thigh. He trailed the whip higher up my leg and over my right hip, my skin tingling from the sensual slide of the leather.

He was close, so close I could feel the warmth of his body, smell the lingering scent of our sex from earlier. He brought his mouth to my ear, his voice a thick whisper of lust.

"Your skin is going to turn such a lovely shade of pink."

I trembled as he ran the leather over my hard nipples, goosebumps forming on my arms.

He stepped away and pulled his arm back, taking the straps with him. I braced myself again as he brought it forward once more, sliding it between my legs, the leather running between my pussy lips like a snake.

I quivered with desire.

He pulled it away again, then lightly hit my thigh with it. He hit it again, harder this time. I bit my lip, holding my breath for the pain that I knew was surely coming.

But it didn't.

The harder he hit, the better it felt.

The pain was a rush of heat to my skin, as if the blow was waking me up with each increase of force. I melted into them, his blows becoming harder and harder until he was raining blows down on me so fast and furiously that they became a blur. My thighs, my belly, my breasts were all tingling with the sensation of being woken up until even the quick rush of air that each blow delivered was like a chorus of pleasure coursing through my veins.

When he stopped, I cried out.

He smiled, a slow approving, proud smile.

"Most people cry when it's happening, not when it stops, Chloe," he whispered, sliding the whip along my trembling skin again. "Tell me, Beauty. Do you like this?" He slipped the leather between my legs, pushing it against my pussy.

I nodded, gasping for breath.

"Good girl," he moaned, reaching down and wrapping his fingers around his cock. "Come down from there."

He unfastened the cuffs on my feet and then my hands. I hadn't realized how weak I was and I sank to the ground, my knees buckling beneath me. I looked back at up him through a curtain of hair. He towered over me, the whip in his hand, his cock pulsing and throbbing between his legs like some sort of virile god of sex.

I'd never wanted to be fucked so badly in my life. I licked my lips, my eyes meeting his, hoping like hell he could see the desire there.

I lifted myself on all fours, crawling towards him, craving the feel of him in my mouth, in my pussy, anywhere and everywhere he could reach.

"Stop!" he commanded. I froze, waiting, a plea of unbridled lust on the tip of my tongue. "Turn around!"

I did as he asked. Walking on my hands and feet in a circle, until my ass was pointed at him. He stepped between my feet, slapping the inside of my thighs with his whip until I opened my thighs wider, my ass and pussy on full display for him.

I pushed away a twinge of shyness, focusing instead on the sweet anticipation. It hit me that this was part of the game. The waiting. The wondering. The imagining.

He walked around to my head and leaned down, staring into my eyes.

His piercing gaze ripped right through me. When he raised his hands, I saw the blindfold. I cringed, the thought of being plunged into darkness, of not being able to see him, to see what he was doing terrified me. I hadn't even imagined he would do that.

When he slipped it over my eyes, I whimpered. Everything turned black and I was left all alone. There was nothing to think about but the darkness and what was coming next.

The fear I'd felt earlier was back. The tiny twinge of anxiety I'd felt before rushed through me, filling my veins, filling every inch of my heart and every dark corner of my mind with white-hot fear.

I waited, relying on my other senses now, to find him, to anticipate what was coming. But suddenly, there was nothing. I couldn't hear him breathing. I couldn't smell him.

Accessing anything but the darkness was impossible.

Was he gone?
Was this part of the game?
A huge mind-fuck of fear?

"Bear?" I called, my voice echoing back to me. I was still on all-fours and I contemplated standing up and feeling my way around. But, still I waited, my ragged breathing the only sound in the room.

"Bear?" I called again, rotating my head. I took another deep breath and reached an arm out in front of me, hitting his abs.

"Oh!" I cried, my finger sliding across his rippling skin.

"I didn't tell you to move," he growled. My hand fell back to the ground and I swallowed hard, letting my head hang down between my arms.

"I thought you left," I whispered.

A hard slap landed on my ass and I jumped and let out a loud yelp.

"Does that feel like I'm gone?" he asked.

"No!" I cried, as he hit me again. His cock brushed against my thigh as his palm landed on my ass cheeks over and over again, until I was whimpering and writhing, my hips dipping down to lessen the blows.

"Stop moving," he said, grabbing me by my waist. He sat down on the nearby chaise and pulled me over his lap, his hard, naked cock pressed against my belly. The spanking began again, harder this time and with nowhere else to go, no way to decrease the impact, I had no choice but to sink into it, just as I had before with the whip.

His hand turned red hot, my ass burning hotter and hotter with each firm slap.

Over and over, the stinging blows echoed through the room. Skin on skin, our bodies sliding together as he kept hitting me. My legs flailed uncontrollably as he continued. Hot tears stung my eyes, sliding from under the blindfold and down my face as I whimpered below him.

"Bear, Bear…" I cried, shaking my head.

He stopped and my stomach flipped.

"Do you want me to stop?" he growled.

"No," I cried. "I want—I want you to fuck me!"

"I'm not ready to fuck you," he said, his cock throbbing hotly against my navel. "You haven't earned that yet, you little slut."

I whimpered again as the purest, strongest desire I'd ever felt rushed through me. To be told no, to be refused his cock when I needed it the most, hurt like nothing I'd felt before. It only made everything worse. It flipped something inside of me and the tears began to flow freely now.

"Please, Bear!" I begged. I didn't care anymore.

"No!" he yelled, his hand landing hard on my ass once more. I hung my head again, falling limp against his lap, taking whatever punishment he thought was best, just wanting him to get it over with so I could feel his cock inside of me again.

I stopped resisting. I let him hit my ass, and after a second, he switched back to the whip. The crack of the leather echoed in the room, mingling with my cries as he hit my thighs, my ass, the whip occasionally falling against my pussy, the blows sending electricity straight to my clit. My juices flowed freely, the wetness seeping onto his thighs, as I lay there, melting into my punishment, taking it like a good girl.

I wanted to please him.

I wanted to hear him call me that again.

It was as if his approval had become my drug, intoxicating me with his game. He hit me again and again, and then he said it, stopping and rubbing his hot hand over the burning stinging flesh of my ass.

"Good girl," he growled. "You take it like a good girl, Chloe…I'm proud of you."

I came in a fit of raw pleasure, my body seized by waves of hot heavenly pain that sent me crashing over the edge of consciousness. His fingers slipped deep inside of me, transporting me into a blissful eden of blackness, ripping my body from this universe and sending me to a starry explosion of lust.

"Bear!" I screamed, his fingers delving deeper as I spasmed around him, my juices bursting forth like a damn had broken loose. He growled above me, pulling his fingers away and then laying me on the chaise on my back.

He shoved his cock inside my spasming pussy, slamming inside of me smoothly, my juices covering us both. My body exploded again, a massive, sweeping wave that left me limp below him as he fucked into me savagely, his hands digging into my hips as he held me in place, his hips flying in the air as he fucked me so hard, so fast, so fucking deep.

I reached up, clawing at the blindfold, desperately wanting to see him.

He slapped my hands away, growled and kept fucking me. Harder and harder his cock slammed into my pussy, fucking me with such precision and strength and intention that every nerve in my body was alive. Harder and harder, faster and faster, until I heard him panting, his breath growing ragged and deep until he stiffened, his cock throbbing and exploding inside of me, his hot wetness filling my pussy as my body seized once more, spasming around him as I cried out his name over and over and over.

"Bear, Bear, Bear…" I cried, tears running down my face.

"Shh, Beauty, shh," he cooed, holding me close, his arms wrapped tightly around me as he kissed my forehead. "You're okay, baby…"

Chapter 23

I awoke in his bed to the sound of the shower running. I stretched my legs and winced, my hand flying down to my ass. It was still hot. It stung like crazy.

In the light of day, laying in his gigantic bed and looking out the window at the view of the city below, things seemed so strange now. We'd gone to bed last night, holding onto each other like we'd found some sort of salvation. And yet, now, in the bright light of day and all alone with nothing but the very real pain that was throbbing through my body, somehow it didn't seem quite so magical.

I'd been drunk last night.

Drunk on the power I'd allowed him to have over me.

Drunk on the relief of letting someone else be in charge.

Drunk on the act of giving my body away to him.

I crawled out of bed, grabbing his robe on a nearby chair and sliding it over my naked, red skin. I looked down at my ass and gasped. Not only was it red, but there were tiny little angry welts all over it and outlines of his fingers that would surely bruise later.

My stomach had bright pink streaks criss-crossing over it, remnants from the leather straps he'd used. My breasts were swollen, my nipples sore from his pinching. I rubbed my wrists, sliding my fingers over the sensitive, raw skin there.

"Jesus," I said, under my breath. I walked out to the terrace, staring down at the city, as I tightened the robe around me, the cold air whipping around my face, tiny snowflakes falling onto my hair.

The people below looked tiny from up here and I couldn't help but wonder if any of them were licking the same sort of wounds as I was this morning.

I couldn't deny that I'd loved it. Every second of it had been filled with this forbidden delight that I'd never experienced before. But I couldn't help but wonder…how far was this going to go? What was his limit?

The rougher he got, the more turned on he was. Fuck, it wouldn't be fair if I didn't admit that I felt the same way. We both enjoyed whatever this was. I didn't have a name for it. I didn't know if he did either.

My mind was spinning as I heard the shower shut off. A minute later, he joined me on the terrace, naked and dripping with tiny beads of water, his hair wet. He smelled like soap and minty toothpaste. I smiled at him, shaking my head as I watched snowflakes land on his eyelashes.

"It's freezing," I said. "You're crazy!"

"I like it," he said, lifting his face to the sky, the snow falling around him. He was a beautiful, magical vision, his perfectly sculpted body looking like something out of a magazine. He smiled and spun around, raising his hands up in the air and laughing. My heart soared as I watched him, amazed at the light that was shining from him in such a purely joyful moment.

Who is he?

He had so many different layers that I couldn't keep up.

I shivered, the flesh on my ass stinging even more out here in the cold. He stopped spinning and closed the distance between us, pulling me into his arms and kissing me. I melted into his warmth, closing my eyes and leaning into his chest as he wrapped his arms around me.

I wanted to stay there forever, the snow drifting around us on his peaceful terrace, high above the frantic pace of the world below.

I had no idea where any of this was going.

I didn't know if this was love.

I had no idea what he was thinking.

I didn't know what our future held.

All I knew was that in that moment, no matter what happened, no matter where I was in a year or a week or even tomorrow, I had—for a brief moment—experienced perfection.

"Let's go inside," he said, breaking the spell. "I have to get to the office."

I sighed and reluctantly followed him in.

"Oh, me too!" I said. "I'll take a quick shower, if that's okay?"

"Sure, but we can't be seen going in to the office together. Max will be waiting outside for you."

"Oh," I said, my heart sinking. After all that stuff last night, part of me thought we'd reached another level. "I see."

He looked at me for a quick second, a flash of something in his eyes that I couldn't quite name, and then he turned and walked into his closet, leaving me standing in his room alone.

"I'll see you at the office," he yelled from the closet. "Lock the door on your way out. Towels are in the top cabinet in the bathroom."

So, that was it?

He was just going to leave me here alone like that? No hug or kiss goodbye? I walked into the bathroom, my heart heavy, feeling like I was doing the walk of shame or something.

I'd let him do things to me last night that I never would have allowed anyone to do—and I'd liked it. It felt so intimate, so personal. I turned on the shower and climbed inside.

When the tears came, I told myself it was because of the pain of the water hitting my raw skin.

By the time I got out of the shower, the tears were gone and so was Bear.

Chapter 24

Massive. That's the only word I could come up with. I'd skipped going into the office, choosing instead to finally take the opportunity to drop by the site of the unfinished hotel. Most of the exterior was finished, but it was missing key elements, like landscaping and lighting, before it would really shine.

When I stepped inside, wearing a hard hat and a name badge that I'd been given by the foreman, I felt like the breath had been ripped from my lungs. It was so big, too big, way too fucking big. I looked straight up through the atrium style tower, the doors of hundreds of rooms looming like one of those unending mirrors in a fun house. I felt sick.

What the hell had I gotten myself into?

I stepped over a pile of tools, lifting my knees up high, which only made the fabric of my wool slacks rub roughly against the welts on my ass. I winced in pain, shaking my head as I tried to take in the scene before me.

I was expected to come up with a cohesive design that would flow perfectly throughout the hotel, starting with the massive lobby, including every single one of the seven different floor plans of guest rooms, the ballrooms, the conference rooms, the endless amount of terraces, the offices, the penthouses and the nightclub located on the very top floor.

Just little old me and my one assistant.

Never mind what was I thinking accepting a job like this, but what the hell was Bear thinking?

All I knew about was sitting in my little studio apartment on Southwest Alder Street in downtown Portland and sewing my little vintage handmade dresses. Where in the hell did all of this come from?

Bear was crazy! I was crazy! This entire town was insane, this entire situation was so out of control. It was too much. That dungeon? What the fuck?

My head spun and I reached out for something to hold onto as the room began spinning. There was nothing around and I'd somehow stupidly convinced the foreman that it was safe to leave me alone in a construction area.

I stumbled outside, gasping for air as I reached the sidewalk, tearing off the hard hat.

Max waited patiently, just as he had every single time I'd needed to go anywhere. He was always around. And so was Bear. Even when he wasn't there, I was drenched in his memory.

Ever since I'd stepped off his plane, I was overwhelmed by him.

And why?

Because he had some warped 'sense' about me when I was still practically a kid?

He'd made me feel things I'd never felt before, but I wasn't sure I was really ready to feel them. How could I give myself away to someone when I didn't fully understand myself yet?

Yes, I was supposed to say yes, but I was starting to think saying yes had gotten me a lot more than I could handle.

My breathing grew shallow and I spun away from Max and began walking down the sidewalk. It took exactly ten steps to realize I had no fucking idea where I was going.

I stopped, took a deep breath and walked back to Max.

"Can you please take me to the library?" I asked.

"Of course, ma'am," he replied, with a curt, professional nod. I'd not given him much thought before, he'd kind of blended into the whole scene that Bear had created. He had a slight accent that I couldn't place and he was darkly handsome, with beautiful olive skin and green eyes. He'd been so quiet.

After he pulled into traffic, I hit the button and the glass slid down.

"Max, where are you from?" I asked.

"Somalia," he said.

"Wow, that's far away from New York," I said.

"It's even further than you think, ma'am," he replied, smiling at me in the rearview mirror.

"Why are you here in New York?" I asked.

"I'm a refugee, ma'am. Mr. Dalton took us in when our family fled the war. I met him when I was working at an elephant sanctuary in Kenya years before we fled. We became friends and when he heard we needed help, he was very generous to my entire family."

"That's wonderful," I said.

"Mr. Dalton is a very good man," he said. "He gave me a job after he helped us get settled here in America. My family and I owe him our lives."

I nodded and smiled, my heart swelling a little. Bear was a good man.

"I'm so glad you're safe," I said. "Thank you for answering. I heard your accent."

"I'm happy you asked. I always welcome an opportunity to talk about my home country and I love singing Mr. Dalton's praises," he said.

I smiled and sat back in the seat, thinking about Bear the whole way to the library. I was impressed with the loyalty that Max felt for him. Bruce seemed to feel the same way to all of his employees. Bear was obviously a good man. He'd not done anything to make me think that he was.

Hell, he had a hell of a lot more faith in me and my abilities than I did. Maybe I just needed to believe in myself more. Maybe what he'd said about believing in yourself was right.

Maybe these were the boundaries I need to push up against.

I vowed not to give up just yet. I'd been close as I'd started to walk down the street back there, but now that I was in the back of the car again, under the watchful protectiveness of Max, I felt a little more stable.

When the car slowed, I looked out the window and gasped.

"The New York Public Library, ma'am," Max said. "The second largest public library in the country! Just call me when you're ready and I'll be here right away.""

"Thank you, Max," I said, staring in awe at the beautiful building in front of me. "I might be a few hours."

I jumped out and was immediately swept up in the sidewalk traffic. It flowed around me like a river and I somehow managed to cross it without getting mowed down. Slowly, I walked up the huge stone steps, in awe of the majesty of the building. Two huge lion statues flanked the steps and people of every size and shape and color swarmed around me, their voices a symphony of a hundred different languages.

My head was swimming, but I managed to make it through the front door, only to be swept up in the awesome beauty of the architecture.

I wandered around for half an hour, lost in the columns and art and hundreds of thousands of books. I passed through exquisitely molded archways that were bordered by huge intricate murals, masterpieces that had stood the test of time, watching over generations of visitors.

Once I'd asked for help finding books on interior design, I got lost in the thousands of books I found. There was so much information I had no idea where to start. I fought to suppress the overwhelming feelings from rushing back and grabbed as many books as I could carry to check out.

By the time I made it back outside, I realized I'd forgotten to call Max. I stumbled to the street with my tower of books, struggling not to slip in the slushy, muddy snow soup that covered every street and sidewalk in this city. I bumped into a man, who reached out and grabbed my arms to help steady me.

"Thank you," I said, looking up at him gratefully. His eyes shifted away quickly. He nodded and kept going.

I took a few more steps, trying desperately not to slip and break my leg. I put the books on a newspaper stand and reached into my purse to search for my phone. I jumped and screamed like a little girl as a rat the size of an alley cat scurried around my foot and through the river of people to the other side.

My heart racing, I took a deep breath, doing my best to calm myself.

You got this, I told myself. Just relax. *All you have to do is call Max and you'll be in the limo, rat-free.*

I fished around in my purse for my phone, reaching past my sunglasses and my keys and lipstick. But no phone.

It wasn't there.

What the fuck? I cried, frantically searching through my purse again.

Nothing.

Wait, *nothing?*

My wallet! *My wallet was gone, too!* I'd just had it when I'd applied for my library card and I'd put it back into my purse, right before I walked outside and bumped into the man.

"No!" I screamed, piercing panic gripping my heart.

The man! He must have pick pocketed me! Maria had warned me about that, but I never thought it was really a thing that happened.

I looked around for Max but there were so many cars and people swirling around I couldn't really focus on any one thing.

What now? I thought. I don't have a phone. No money, no bank cards. At least my house keys were still in my pocket, but I didn't even know how to walk back home from here.

I'd never felt so lost in my life.

What the hell was I doing here? I thought. This wasn't me, this wasn't my life. This was someone else's life. I didn't belong here. I had no idea how to get around, how to even live here without the help of someone else.

I missed my independence. I missed my home town. I missed my friends, my apartment, my sense of fucking direction.

Grabbing the books, I took off walking. I figured if I just kept walking with the flow of traffic, maybe I'd see something I recognized, or I'd figure out a solution eventually. But Max and Bear had driven me everywhere since I'd arrived and I'd not paid much attention at all to my surroundings.

So dumb! I thought, as I stumbled through the slush. *What was I thinking?*

The sound of a horn blaring made me almost jump out of my skin.

"Miss McDonnell?" I heard a voice yell. I looked towards it and almost started crying when I saw Max creeping up next to me. "Miss McDonnell, get in, I can't pull over here!"

I ran over to him and jumped in the back seat, my books falling to my feet.

"Max!" I cried, "Thank you!"

"Miss, I'm so sorry, I thought you were going to call me. The NYPD doesn't let us wait outside the library anymore."

"I lost my phone!" I said. "Well, I think it was stolen, actually. My wallet is gone, too."

"Oh, no! The grifters have been bad this year, I heard."

"I'm just so glad to see you!" I said. "I didn't know what I was going to do."

"Well, you're safe now. Do you want to go home now?"

"Yes, please," I said, sinking back into the seat breathlessly, thanking my lucky stars he'd seen me. "Thank you again, Max."

"My pleasure, miss."

* * *

My afternoon consisted of a three hour trip to the DMV to get a new ID and another hour spent on the phone canceling my credit cards. By the time I was done, my day was shot.

Later that night, I was pouring over the books I'd checked out, feeling like a total fraud. I didn't really even know the difference between art deco or art nouveau. And there was so much to learn!

Bohemian, Industrial, Mid-Century Modern, Nautical, Scandinavian, Farmhouse, Urban Modern, Shabby Chic, it went on and on and on. After hours of research, I still had no clue which direction to go in.

With all the other confusion I was experiencing when it came to Bear, I was ready to hang up my hat.

You just have to tell him, I told myself. Tell him it's too much, the job, his fetish, his fucking dungeon. I guess that's what it was, right? A fetish. It's not like he was licking my toes and asking me to have sex in a park so everyone could see. I mean, not yet. Who knew what was coming at this point? But this was definitely not normal, as far as I could tell.

I laid on my bed, staring up at the ceiling, trying to make sense of it all.

It wasn't that everything I'd experienced wasn't amazing and eye-opening. But this was Bear's life and I was merely playing a part in it. I hadn't gone out seeking these bruises on my ass. I hadn't asked him to tie me up or to blindfold me or to use those whips on me or to do any of those things.

I'd not asked for any of it. Maybe that's why I wasn't sure if this was right for me. I'd never even had a spanking fantasy before I met Bear. Maybe if I had more time to think about it, to develop an appreciation for it a little more slowly.

How in the world did he ever see something in myself that I didn't know existed?

How was that possible?

My phone buzzed next to me and I saw it was Marie calling. I sighed, throwing the phone back on the bed. I didn't have the energy to talk to her right now. She was always so sure of herself, so confident and happy. The last thing I needed was to hear her chipper cheerleading.

I don't know what I needed, really.

Maybe I needed to just buck up and believe in myself, but that was hard to do when you were just plopped into a job you knew nothing about.

Or, maybe, just maybe, I needed to cut my losses.

Tuck tail and head home.

Home to the rain and my friends and all the tree lined streets that I knew like the back of my hand. Maybe I'd be happier if I went home to everything that was familiar and easy and real.

My phone beeped to tell me Marie left a voicemail. I hit the button to listen to it and her voice began chirping through my room.

"Hey girl, where are you?" she said. "I know your phone is right there next to you, unless of course, you're preoccupied with that beasty Bear of yours! Listen, I just wanted to give you a heads up. Jessica's friend Sally mentioned to Harlan that you moved to New York. Apparently, he's pissed you left without telling him. He might be on his way to find you. Anyway, watch your back, okay? I don't trust that guy. Call me when you can. Love you!"

Silence filled my room as the voicemail shut off. Harlan's face flashed in my head and I groaned. The last thing I needed was to be forced to deal with him. Luckily, this city was massive and he wasn't going to be able to just find me down at the corner pub like he would in Portland. I wasn't too worried about him. I was pretty sure he'd have given up on me by now, but I guess some people take a little more time than others.

My phone buzzed again and I groaned, thinking it would be Marie again, but it wasn't.

It was Bear.

"Hey," I answered.

"Beauty!" he said. "I just inked a huge deal and I want to celebrate!"

"Celebrate?" I asked, looking at the clock. It was past nine.

"Yes!" he said. "Put your party dress on, baby! I'll pick you up in half an hour!"

"Half an—," the phone clicked and he was gone.

Jesus! What if I didn't want to go dancing? I'd already had a few glasses of wine, I was in my pajamas and totally looking forward to a warm night of snuggling up and feeling sorry for myself.

"Shit," I muttered, getting out of bed and heading to the closet. I pulled out a sparkly cocktail dress I'd bought, some shimmering tights and a pair of stilettos. I got dressed, remembering to keep the panties in the drawer and went to the bathroom to try to make sense of my hair and makeup.

I was puffy, I'd been crying and I looked like I'd just lost my best friend.

"Perk up, buttercup!" I said to the mirror. I took a deep breath, sprayed dry shampoo all over my hair and put it up in a bun. Luckily, the makeup covered up all traces of the sad girl from before and I grabbed a coat and waited for Bear to arrive.

Chapter 25

The club was insanely loud, the techno music pumping through the place and sending sickening bass sounds straight to my gut. Bear grabbed my hand and led me to a back room that by the looks of the way it was separated from the rest of the place, meant it was probably a VIP area.

We sat in a booth overlooking the rest of the club and he ordered drinks when the waitress appeared. I couldn't hear a thing they said, though, and all I could do was hope he ordered water for me, instead of something alcoholic.

The crowd was huge, and the dance floor was small, making for a very entertaining situation to watch as people tried to dance without running into each other. It didn't work.

Most people danced with their hands waving in the air, leaving their boobs and butts and everything else fair game to be rubbed up on.

I turned to Bear and screamed.

"Do you come here often?" I asked.

"What?" he screamed back.

"You come here a lot?" I yelled again.

"Did you ask if I like tator-tots?" he yelled.

I rolled my eyes. This was useless. I shook my head and gave up any attempt at conversation. He shrugged and smiled, putting his hand on my thigh and brushing a kiss across my cheek.

The waitress came back and I cringed when I saw her set an entire bottle of champagne in front of us. I guess Bear really did want to celebrate. He'd told me a little about the deal he'd closed today in the car on the way over. It was some huge office building in Brooklyn that had been fraught with complications of every kind that he'd been trying to work through for years. Today, he'd finally gotten through all the red tape and it was his to do with as he pleased.

I watched him pour the foamy, bubbly liquid in two glasses and he handed one to me. I smiled, watching as he held up his own glass in a toast.

He said something about a building and the future but that's all I could make out before he clinked my glass and downed his champagne in one shot. I sipped mine slowly, knowing it would hit me quickly.

Champagne only affected me in one of two ways—it either made me very happy and giggly or it made me puke. The fact that I'd already consumed wine made me pretty sure where things were headed if I drank too much now.

Instead, I watched as Bear got drunk. I couldn't say anything, because he was so happy, but why would I anyway? It wasn't my place to say anything. He wasn't driving.

And, he was celebrating. He seemed so happy.

So, I sat there, doing what I thought I should be doing. We couldn't talk to each other because of the music and he wasn't making any move to dance, so I sat there, pretending to drink my champagne and smiling at him occasionally. Despite the fact that he hadn't answered my question, it was obvious this was definitely not his first time here. At least six different women and three men came up to greet him. Each one leaned down, whispering in his ear and patting him on the back. I tried to ignore the gushing cheek kisses pressed to his face and the side glances that were thrown my way once they saw me sitting next to him and nobody tried to talk to me.

Finally, I got up to go to the ladies room, leaving him in the booth alone with his champagne and his endless stream of friends.

The line for the ladies room was out the door. I groaned and got in line behind a statuesque blonde with a skimpy red dress on. When she turned around, I realized it was the same girl from the steakhouse—Zoe Rothchild.

She recognized me immediately.

"Oh, it's you!" she said. "I'm surprised to see you again."

"Hello," I said, my voice cold as ice. I'd already decided I hated her the first time.

"So, did it happen?" she asked.

"Did what happen?"

"Bear, of course. I warned you about him. Did he break your heart yet?"

"No," I said. "We're just friends."

"Oh, please!" she laughed. "Bear isn't just friends with any woman. Don't forget what I said, little one," she winked, "Bear Dalton will eat you alive!"

"I'm looking forward to it," I replied, lifting my chin.

Fuck her, I thought. *Who does she think she is? I don't even know her and she thinks she can say these things to me?*

She laughed again and then raked her eyes up and down my body.

"You aren't his usual type," she said, wrinkling her perfect little button nose. I suppressed a sudden urge to punch it. "Maybe you'll stick around a little longer than the others."

"But others, do you mean you, Zoe?" I asked.

"Oh, you're a little firecracker, aren't you?" she said, raising an eyebrow.

"Maybe I'm just not intimidated by women like you."

"No?" she asked, putting a perfectly manicured finger up to her lips mockingly. "Well, good for you. Bear needs a woman who can take a lot of punishment."

She turned away and walked into the stall, leaving me stand there, my heart racing, my face flushed. Another stall opened up and I walked in, locking the door behind me and falling into it. I didn't care how long it took, I planned on staying in there until I was sure Zoe was gone. She was so creepy and her words sliced right through me.

How many people knew about Bear's tendencies for rough sex? Did everyone know? Was I just one more notch on the wall of his dungeon?

I waited a good ten minutes, looking under the stalls for Zoe's sky high red pumps. I didn't see them, so I left the bathroom, slowly making my way back to Bear and keeping an eye out for Zoe at the same time. I was done talking to that bitch.

My heart sank when I saw her sitting in my seat next to Bear, the two of them laughing together. I started to turn away and leave them alone when I heard Bear call my name. I froze and turned back to see the two of them smiling at me and Bear gesturing for me to come back.

Deep breath, I reminded myself as I put one foot in front of the other. I plastered a fake smile on my face and nodded to them as I approached.

"Chloe, I want you to meet a dear friend of mine, Zoe Rothchild. Zoe, this is Chloe, she's going to be designing my new hotel."

She smiled and held out her hand. I reached out, shaking it, my stomach flipping in disgust.

"Chloe, that's a big job," she said. *Don't remind me*, I thought.

"Yes, I'm looking forward to it," I lied. In fact, I was lying so hard that I was surprised my pants hadn't caught on fire. Oh, right, I wasn't wearing any. In fact, I wasn't wearing panties either. But still, if I was, there would have been flames. That's how much I wasn't looking forward to this job.

"I'm sure you'll do a tremendous job," she said. She reached over and put her hand over Bear's and squeezed, flashing the fakest, whitest, widest smile I'd ever seen. I could have sown I saw a little sparkle flash from her teeth. "Working with Bear is a delight!"

"Yes, it is," I replied, meeting her gaze daringly, shooting daggers into her with my eyes. "Have you had the pleasure?"

"Me?" she asked, throwing a teasing glance at Bear. "Well, yes, we've done a little business together."

"Zoe is a designer herself, Chloe. She led the design team that worked on my first hotel ten years ago. We go way back. We met back in Yale."

"Oh," I said, my heart sinking as I watched the two of them stare admiringly at one another. "I see."

"So, what are you?" she asked, looking back at me. " Pratt? Parsons? Cornell?"

"Excuse me?" I asked.

"Where did you get your degree, Chloe?"

"Oh. Portland State," I replied.

"Oh," she said, raising an eyebrow. "That's so cute! How quaint!"

My eyes landed on her perfect little beak once more. It was now raised so high up in the air I could see up it. I clenched my fists at my sides and realized that I'd never felt the need to actually punch someone before. Instead, I smiled at her silently, not bothering with a response to her thinly veiled insult.

"I should be going, Bear," she said, kissing him again on the cheek. "I'm redesigning The Mark Hotel, did you hear?"

"I did not! Congratulations, dear," he said, standing up as she did.

"Talk to you soon," she said, turning to me and winking. "Nice to meet you, Chloe."

I nodded, speechless.

The balls on that woman, I thought as I sat back down. I grabbed my glass of champagne and downed it. Bear looked at me curiously and smiled as he poured more in my glass.

"Want to dance?" he asked. I looked down at the crowded dance floor and shook my head.

"Not really," I said. "Actually, can we get out of here? It's a little too crowded. I could use some air."

He reached over and squeezed my thigh, his warm hand sliding up under my skirt. He brushed his fingers against my bare pussy and nodded approvingly.

"That's sounds like a good idea," he said, "as soon as we finish this bottle!"

He turned and poured more champagne, drinking it quickly. I looked at the bottle and was equally delighted and dismayed that it was almost all gone. He'd drank a lot. And by the pulsing in my temples, I'd had a little too much myself.

But all I could think about was getting out of there, so I grabbed the bottle and poured the rest in my glass, downing it quickly.

"Now?" I asked.

"Wow, you weren't kidding," he laughed, grabbing his coat.

We trailed out of the club, which took twice as long as it normally would, because he stopped every few minutes to say goodbye to someone. To my relief, Zoe wasn't anywhere in sight.

By the time we got back in the car, my head was throbbing.

"Well, that was fun, wasn't it?" he asked, reaching for another drink from the bar.

"Sure," I said, clutching my temples.

"You don't seem like your normal self," he remarked.

My normal self? I thought. What did that even look like? All of this was so far out of my usual self that I'd forgotten what normal actually looked like.

"I guess I'm just a little tired," I said, trying to muster a smile. The truth was that seeing Zoe again had shaken me. Now that I'd seen Bear at his darkest, seen his secret dungeon, for lack of a better word, seen the side of him that I thought he didn't show most people, I thought we had something special.

Zoe had managed to rip that all away in just a few words.

"Tired? But, Beauty, the night is still young!" he said, as he reached forward and pushed the button, the glass between us and his driver sliding down.

"Take us to the Empire State Building, please, Max," he said.

"Yes, sir," Max said.

"What!" I said. "Bear, it's so late."

"You haven't been, have you? It's open until two in the morning, love. You'll love it! Trust me! It's beautiful this time of night!"

"Okay, okay," I relented, suppressing a yawn. More than anything, I wanted to go home. I wanted to think about everything, make sense of stuff that didn't make sense to me yet.

We were silent on the drive. He kept drinking in the car, lost in his own thoughts. But by the time we arrived, he perked up, his eyes flashing with excitement.

"I haven't been here in years!" he said. "The elevator ride alone is amazing."

He grabbed my hand and pulled me inside. I waited while he bought tickets and when the elevator doors opened, we walked in first. We stood in the back while a few other people walked on.

Once the door closed, I jumped when I felt his hand slid up the back of my skirt. We were standing against the back wall of the elevator, out of view of everyone else, and my eyes widened when his fingers slid up and pressed against my naked ass. He slipped inside my asshole and I bit my lip to keep from crying out. I turned my head to look at him, but he stood staring straight ahead, as if his hand was half buried in my ass, his finger fucking in and out of me.

When the elevator dinged, he slid out and pulled the back of my skirt down as the people in front of us walked out. I looked back at him and he winked, grabbing my arm and leading me away from all the people.

"Come this way," he said. "I want to show you something."

He opened a door that led outside, a blast of cold air hitting us as soon as we stepped out. The city sparkled below us and we walked around the open observation deck that was lined with coin-operated telescopes.

"This is incredible!" I said, the wind blowing my hair around me.

"Isn't it?" he asked, as he led me around the deck. "I knew you'd love it."

"I do, Bear! It's stunning!" The freezing wind had woken me up, all traces of sleepiness having vanished as soon as we stepped out into it.

"Look over there," he finally stopped and pointed in the distance. "Lady Liberty herself!"

"Oh! That's the first time I've seen her since I've been here," I said.

"And look over there," he pointed somewhere else. "That's your apartment building."

"Oh, I see it!" I said, squinting to try to make sense of the millions of lights laid out in front of us.

"Now, walk around here," he said, leading me away again. I followed him, hand in hand until he stopped abruptly and turned around to face me. We were alone, with no other people in sight.

He let go of my hand and reached down, unzipping his pants and pulling out his rock hard cock.

"Suck it," he growled.

"What? Here, Bear?" I asked, already shaking my head no.

"On your fucking knees, Chloe!" he said, his voice low and seething.

"But Bear—," I began to protest.

He reached up and grabbed my head, pulling me into him and kissing me hard on the mouth.

"Shut the fuck up!" he growled. "Suck my cock now!"

"What about the people?" I cried, my pussy twitching with excitement.

"I don't care about them. I don't care if they see you sucking my cock, Chloe. I want your mouth and I want it right this fucking instant, do you fucking hear me?"

I sighed with dismay, looking over my shoulder before sinking to my knees in front of him.

"Mmm, good girl," he whispered, stroking my hair as I slid his cock inside of my mouth. "That's it, baby, that's so good."

His words shot right through me, waking up that part of me that I'd been so unable to access earlier. I was so worried about the job, about not knowing what I was doing, about trying to figure him out and figure out what all of this meant, that I couldn't focus on the way he made me feel. I'd been worrying way too much.

Until now.

His cock slid back and forth between my lips, the skin so soft and velvety and hard, all at the same time, his throbbing, pulsing sex coming to life in my mouth. I moaned, twirling my tongue around the head and sucking him in hard, my hand reaching up and gripping his shaft.

I melted into the act, but at the same time, I was terrified of getting caught. *Don't people get arrested for stuff like this?* I wondered. I couldn't imagine the security guards took too lightly to people fucking up here. We were in a dark corner and while we hadn't yet been discovered, once again, just like on the trail, I could hear faint voices approaching. I moved faster, sucking harder, swirling my tongue around him as fast as I could, hoping he would come quickly and we could finish this somewhere a lot warmer and much more private.

He had other ideas, though.

"Stand up," he commanded, pulling his cock from my grip.

I stood up, ignoring the pain in my knees from kneeling. I met his gaze and saw the fiery passion there that I'd come to love. Something stirred in me, as if he was creating a storm inside of me and churning it up into some kind of furious wild abandon that gripped my soul.

He turned me around, his hands on my waist as he pushed me up against a window. He reached down, pulling my skirt up around my hips and exposing my bare ass and pussy to all of New York City.

"Isn't this exciting?" he growled. "You could get caught at any moment, Chloe, then everyone will know what a slut you are."

I groaned, my pussy spasming at his words, my nipples hardening into tiny little pebbles of forbidden arousal.

His hand landed smartly on my ass, smacking it hard before he plunged his cock inside of my pussy. I was already wet. So fucking wet. And within seconds, I was writhing on his hardness, loving the delicious smooth slide of his piercing cock. He reached up and grabbed my hair, pulling my head back as he fucked into me. His other hand reached into the top of my dress, pulling out my breasts and pinching my nipples hard.

I cried out, unable to stay quiet during his relentless fucking. I spasmed around his shaft, coming hard and quick, pulsing around him as he pistoned in and out of me.

"Good girl," he growled in my ear. "Yes, Chloe, come on my cock, that's it, baby."

I came hard, again and again, as he continued fucking me.

I was just catching my breath when I felt him pull out. I thought he was finished and started to raise myself up, but his hand landed on the middle of my back and he pushed me back down.

"I'm not done," he said. My eyes flew open as I felt the head of his cock press against my asshole. I shook my head frantically.

"I don't think I can do that, Bear," I cried, looking over my shoulder at him.

"Yes you can," he said, pressing forward. I whimpered, completely bewildered as to why he would attempt something like this here, on top of the Empire State Building, of all places.

I'd never been fucked in the ass before, not officially. Sure, I'd had fingers and vibrators, but that is nothing compared to a live, hard cock, as I was about to discover.

I felt the pain immediately.

Burning, searing, white-hot pain flashed through my body as he slid inside of me.

"Bear!" I cried, doing my best to stay still.

He began thrusting in and out of my ass slowly and at first, I couldn't believe how much it hurt. Hot, stinging tears welled up in my eyes.

"Oh, baby, baby," he growled behind me, kissing my neck. "You're so fucking tight. So warm. So fucking perfect." He reached around me, finding my clit and slowly rubbing it as he slowly fucked in and out of me. Within seconds of him touching my clit, the pain began to change into hot waves of pleasure bubbling up inside of me, my pussy once again flowing like a river.

A deep moan escaped from my lips, the pain fading away completely until I was writhing in the purest pleasure, my body pressed up against the window as he pounded into my ass. Savage, raw, delicious passion ripped through me, turning every nerve in my body into a symphony of bliss that took over my entire soul, until I was coming again, my body seizing up around him as he continued to fuck into me. He swelled bigger and hotter inside of me, his cock throbbing as he exploded, his hot seed spilling out, burning me with his sweet release.

He fell against my back, panting, his cock sliding out of me, leaving me yearning for more. I moaned, turning my face back to his.

"That was incredible," I said, my eyes wide with wonder.

"Better than the view?" he asked, a sly smile on his face. I pulled my skirt down and turned around as he pushed his cock back into his pants and zipped them up.

"Much better than the view," I whispered, a sense of something I couldn't quite name rushing over me.

Was it love? It felt like love. It felt like I'd never felt before. My heart was full and all I wanted to do was fall into his arms. I'd never done that before and I'd certainly never expected that to happen in a place like this, let alone with a man like him.

Suddenly, I felt so vulnerable. I wanted him to hold me. I wanted him to kiss me gently and tell me everything really did make sense, even if it didn't seem that way.

But he didn't. He turned away, taking in the view, as if he hadn't just plunged himself into my most sacred place.

"Let's go," he said, walking away from me, his gait a little unsteady. Silently, I followed him, studying his back for some sign of emotion.

Nothing.

We got back in the elevator and he didn't touch me the entire ride back down. When we got back in the limo, he sat opposite me, reaching for more champagne.

I sighed, shifting gingerly. Between the bruises and welts still on my skin and the pounding he had just given my ass, I was pretty proud of the fact that I wasn't crying out from all the pain. Now that he wasn't inside of me, the pleasure had faded and the wincing and stinging was back in full force.

"How well do you know Zoe?" I asked, my words seeming to come from out of nowhere. I certainly hadn't planned on letting them escape my stupid brain, but they fell out like a bunch of oranges from a shopping bag.

"Zoe?" he asked, confusion filling his eyes.

"Yes," I asked, staring over at him. He squinted a second, then cocked his head.

"Why do you ask?"

"She seems to know a lot about you," I remarked.

"She does?" he asked.

"Sure," I said. "Did she tell you I met her in the bathroom? That wasn't the first time, either. I saw her the first time at that steak house we went to."

"She didn't tell me any of that," he shook his head. "What did she say to you? She can be a bit of a bitch sometimes."

"She said you would eat me alive," I said, raising my chin.

His laughter echoed through the limo and he slapped his knee.

"She told you that, did she?" he said, gasping for air.

"I'm glad you think that's funny," I said.

"Don't you?"

"No, not particularly," I said.

"Surely, you aren't jealous of Zoe Rothchild, are you?" he said.

"What place do I have to be jealous of anyone?" I said, spitting out the words. Anger began welling up in side of me. Maybe it was because I was feeling so lost, so vulnerable. Maybe I just needed answers. Maybe none of this was for me and I didn't have the skills to handle it.

"What do you mean by that?" he asked.

"Never mind," I shook my head, looking away from him. I didn't want any part of his piercing gaze. I didn't want him to look right through me anymore. I didn't want him to see my confusion, my uncertainty, my self-doubt. I hated being vulnerable.

I wanted him to see a sophisticated woman, like Zoe, when he looked at me. So far, I was pretty sure that wasn't happening.

"Chloe," he said. "Look at me."

"Forget I said anything," I replied, refusing to look his way. The limo pulled up in front of my apartment building and I took a deep breath. Putting my hand on the door handle, I turned back to look at him finally.

He looked confused and lost and buzzed.

"Chloe, what's going on?" he asked.

"I can't do this," I said.

"Do what, darling?"

I shook my head, his beautiful dark eyes staring back at me, and I knew this moment would probably haunt me forever.

"This, Bear, I can't do this. All of it."

"Is it the job? Chloe, we can find something else for you to do, if you want."

"It's the job, yes. But it's more than that. I can't do this right now. I don't even know what I'm doing!"

"Chloe, calm down. Everything is going to be fine."

"No, it isn't!" I cried. "I don't even know who you are, Bear. One minute, you're gentle and loving and the next minute you're acting like I'm some whore you picked up in Times Square!"

"They don't have whores in Times Square anymore," he said, smiling.

I crossed my arms and looked away, shaking my head.

"Chloe, come on—," he began, reaching for me.

I put out a hand and shook my head.

"No, Bear," I said.

I got out of the car and stood on the sidewalk, staring down at him in the limo. I shook my head, my heart in my throat.

"I'm sorry, Bear," I said, my voice quivering with emotion.

"Chloe, let's talk about this."

"Peaches."

"What!" he yelled. "Chloe! Come on!"

I shook my head and walked away, tears spilling down my face.

Chapter 26

I sat on my terrace the next morning, a hot cup of coffee in my hands, as I listened to the sounds of the city below. Horns blowing, people yelling, car tires skidding and garbage trucks clanking, the song of the city echoing down the street and up into the air.

It was barely six a.m. and all this was going on below already.

I'd woken before dawn after crying myself to sleep, my dreams haunted by Bear's face.

Now, in the light of day, the world seemed a little clearer. Now that I was alone and had some space and time to think, my decision seemed obvious.

Coming here to New York had been a whirlwind of unexpected adventures. I was beyond grateful for the opportunity to experience every minute.

But everything about New York was harsh and extreme. From the weather to the people, to the pace, to the expectations that had been put on me. I was a lily-white, thin-skinned, lightweight of a human. I'm sensitive. My heart is huge and open and raw.

How was I supposed to survive these conditions with this kind of disposition?

It's not that I'm not strong.

I am really fucking strong. But this just isn't me.

I'm strong, but I'm soft, too.

New York City is as hard as a diamond, with not a soft space to land in sight. I just couldn't understand it. I couldn't wrap myself around it. And I needed that in a home. I needed a place, a person, a home that I could melt into.

I'd thought maybe I'd found that in Bear. But he was just too much of everything—he was just like the city that had raised him. A big giant ball of tension and drama and intrigue and shock that never let up. I never had time to catch my breath around him. It had become almost impossible to relax.

And, now, more than ever, I wanted to relax. I wanted familiarity. I wanted friends and dive bars and rain.

More than anything, I wanted things to be clear.

Bear clouded my mind beyond belief.

I couldn't have both. It was time to be honest with myself.

I finished my coffee and went into the bedroom, pulling my suitcase out of the closet. I packed slowly, my hands running over all the beautiful clothes he'd bought me as I put them away. When I was done, I walked into the spare bedroom that Bear had turned into my studio.

I'd not used it once the whole time.

I'd hardly been home at all, actually.

I trailed my hand over the brand new sewing machine, smiling wistfully at it.

"We could have had a lot of fun together," I said, feeling a twinge of guilt that I'd never even turned it on. Bear was a good man. He was special and thoughtful and generous.

But he was so much more, more than I could handle. He may have seen something in me, but whatever it was, it wasn't ready for the intensity that he brought to the table.

I turned off the light and closed the door, walking back to my bedroom to grab my phone. Sitting down, I pulled up the travel app and booked the next flight to Portland.

Chapter 27

"Mom," I said into her voicemail, "I can't make lunch today. Don't be mad, but I'm going back to Portland. My flight leaves in two hours. I'll call you when I arrive. I'm sorry, I tried, but New York just isn't for me."

I hung up, so happy she hadn't actually answered the phone. I didn't want to argue with her and I certainly didn't want to explain everything to her. There weren't enough lies that I could come up with right now to make anything I said sound normal.

I'm leaving because your billionaire boss made me his sex slave and took my ass virginity at the top of the Empire State Building and I don't know how to emotionally process all of this shit?

Yeah, it didn't sound like something one should say to a parent, did it?

I grabbed my bag, my stack of library books and left the keys and Bear's credit card on the kitchen counter. My stomach dropped as I closed the door for the last time. I made my way down to the security desk and asked the security guy if he would please return the books for me. I was so thankful he agreed, because the thought of trying to figure out how to get back to the library on my own was not a pleasant one.

I walked outside to hail a cab and ran right into Max.

"Ready to go meet Ms. Matilda for lunch, ma'am?" he asked.

"Oh, Max! I forgot to tell you, I'm so sorry. I won't need you today. I'm not going to lunch with my Mom after all. In fact, I won't need you at all anymore. But thank you, you've been so helpful and kind."

"Won't need me at all? Why not, ma'am?," he asked.

"I'm going back to Portland."

"Oh?" he asked. "Mr. Dalton didn't mention it to me."

"He doesn't really know yet," I said. "I just decided this morning."

He looked at me, squinting his eyes curiously.

"Oh, I see," he nodded.

"Thank you, again, Max. I'll just hail a taxi to the airport."

"Oh, no, ma'am. Please let me take you."

"That's okay," I refused.

"No, I insist. Mr. Dalton would be so upset if I let you go in a taxi."

I sighed, looking into his kind eyes.

"Okay, then," I relented, "thank you, Max."

"It is absolutely my pleasure!" he said, opening the door. He took my bag and put it in the trunk and slid behind the wheel. The glass was already down and I was grateful for it. I didn't want to be alone right now.

The car pulled away from the curb and Max looked at me in the mirror.

"What is Portland like?" he asked.

"Portland? You've never been?" I asked, thinking about it. "It's—well, it's kind of dreary, actually. It rains about nine months out of the year."

"That sounds awful," he said.

"I guess so. You get used to it."

"When I first moved to New York," he said, "I hated it. I couldn't believe people lived in such a crowded place. I was particularly offended by the rats. They seemed so big and they were everywhere."

"That's how I felt the first time I visited," I agreed.

"But you know what?" he asked. "Now, I don't even notice them. I'm just like everyone else, just going about my business and ignoring them. I used to shudder in disgust every time I saw one. It's amazing what you can get used to in time."

I nodded, thinking about what he was saying. He was right. I'd gotten used to quite a lot in my life. I'd gotten used to not having a father. I'd gotten used to my absentee mother. I'd gotten used to the rain and dreary skies.

"I suppose one could get used to almost anything," I said.

"It's true," Max nodded.

We were silent for a few minutes, before he spoke up again.

"Mr. Dalton will not be happy you are leaving," he said.

"You don't think so?" I asked. "I guess he'll get used to that, too, won't he?"

"Maybe," he replied, "but maybe not."

"I think he'll be okay," I said.

"He's a strong man, sure," he said, thoughtfully, "but still, there's something different about him when he's with you. He lights up in a way I've never seen. Like something in him comes alive that he usually keeps hidden away in the dark."

I nodded, speechless, my eyes stinging with tears.

We didn't talk the rest of the way. I had no idea how to respond anyway and I was thankful he didn't press the issue. There was something very special about Max and I realized I was going to miss him.

He pulled up to the drop off point at the airport and came around to open the door.

I stood on the sidewalk with my bags and put my hand out to shake his. He looked at my outstretched hand and smiled, before pulling me in for a hug and kissing my cheek.

"In Somalia, that is how we say goodbye to our friends."

I smiled up at him.

"Thank you again, Max," I said. "Take care of yourself."

"I hope to see you again very soon, ma'am," he said.

I nodded, a huge empty pit growing in the bottom of my stomach as I walked away and into the airport, leaving New York City and everything and everyone in it, far, far behind.

Chapter 28

I sat at the gate, mindlessly scrolling through Facebook on my phone. My plane was half an hour late and we hadn't even boarded yet. It had taken forever to get through security and they'd looked through my entire bag, pulling out all the fancy lingerie I'd bought and pouring it out on the floor.

I was so embarrassed and I'd wished I'd left it all behind.

It's not like I was ever going to wear it again. My heart was already hurting just thinking about it. I was giving up everything. I was blowing the biggest opportunity I'd ever been given. And I was probably going to end up throwing away the most expensive lingerie I'd ever buy in my life after only wearing it once.

Was I an idiot?

Was I making a huge mistake letting fear and confusion send me fleeing to safety?

Sure, of course I was.

But that was the decision I'd made and I was determined to go through with it. I'd look really stupid if I turned back now. I had to make a decision and stick to it and this was the only one I was brave enough to make.

I stopped scrolling when I saw a status update from Harlan.

In usual Facebook style, it was something that he'd posted two days ago and just now popped up in my feed.

She can block me but she can't hide. Nobody runs from Harlan. I'm coming to catch you, Chloe.

I shuddered as I read through the comments. Thankfully, it was a group of our mutual friends calling him out on being incredibly creepy and stalker-ish. I could only hope one of them had gotten through to him. I'd barely given him a second thought since I'd blocked his number on my phone. I hadn't thought to block him on Facebook. I'd been so preoccupied with Bear that Harlan was the last person on my mind.

An overhead voice announced my plane was boarding and I sighed with relief. Sitting at the airport waiting felt like being in limbo. It was torturous and took all my strength not to just give in and run back to Bear's arms. Because the truth was, I didn't know what I was doing. I didn't know if this was the right thing to do or if leaving was something I would regret for the rest of my life.

All I knew for certain was that Bear Dalton shook me to my very core and I had no idea how to handle that.

It was simple, actually.

I stood up and got in line, thankful that I was finally going to be out of here in a few minutes. I looked out the window at the huge jet that would carry me back home and had a flash of memory of my flight here.

I smiled when I remembered the note Bear had sent me telling me take off my panties. It had all seemed like such innocent fun and games back then. I had no idea what was in store for me back then. My heart soared as I thought about how it had all felt. I'd been so nervous and yet so excited, like a little kid going to Disneyland.

The unknown had excited me. The thought of getting to know Bear had excited me.

His brazenness had excited me.

And now, here I was—afraid of it. Filled with fear because I didn't know how far he could go, how far I could go — how far I wanted it to go.

Oh, how the mighty have fallen, I thought.

I thought about that girl back then and I admired her courage. She seemed fearless to me. Where had that girl gone? What happened to saying yes?

Had she really been so frightened that she'd lost her backbone completely?

I waited in line, a sense of shame washing over me.

I should have been stronger, I thought. I should have given it more time. I should have bucked up and believed in myself.

Instead, I was here in this line, one slow-as-molasses step closer to failure as the line moved forward. I fought back the tears as disappointment filled my heart.

Finally, I handed my boarding pass to the attendant. She looked at it and handed it back to me with a smile.

"Enjoy your flight," she said. I resisted the urge to scoff at her and took a deep breath, walking away.

I'd taken three steps when I heard someone call my name.

Chapter 29

I turned to see Bear running towards me.

"Fuck!" I muttered, shaking my head.

"Chloe!" he yelled. "Stop! Please!"

He rushed towards me, ignoring the attendant and closing the distance between us. He looked disheveled, his deep blue eyes filled with sadness and confusion.

He looks like I feel, I thought.

"Chloe, what are you doing?" he asked, staring down at me.

"I'm going home, Bear. I'm sorry I didn't tell you. I just couldn't."

"Why are you doing this? This is your home now."

"No," I said, shaking my head, my heart breaking. "It's not."

"Chloe," he pleaded. "Let's talk. Just give me five minutes."

I sighed and nodded.

"Okay, but I can't miss my flight," I said, moving away from the entrance and walking with him over to the window. The jet loomed, waiting to take me home.

"Chloe, I was a complete and utter asshole last night, I'm so sorry. I shouldn't have had so much to drink and I should have been gentler with you. It's all my fault. I got carried away celebrating."

"It's not that," I said, even though it was a little bit. But people were watching us and the last thing I wanted to do was talk about him taking my ass in public.

"What is it, then?" he asked.

"It's everything else, Bear. I don't know how to do that job you want me to do. I'm clueless. And I just don't understand what's happening. Between us. With us. None of this makes sense."

"Don't you see?" he said, his voice gentle and soft. "This thing between us makes perfect sense."

"How is that?" I asked. "Look, Bear, I'm not whatever you think I am. You can find someone else to fulfill those needs. You'd be better off with a woman like Zoe. Someone who fits your lifestyle."

"Zoe?" he scoffed. "She's a fragile fucking butterfly that I hate being around."

"Well, whomever…" I said, my voice trailing off.

"Chloe, listen to me. Look at me!" he said. My eyes darted up, hypnotized by his piercing glare. "I thought I made myself clear the other day, but maybe not. I have never in my life met a woman like you. You're special, don't you see? I've tried being with other people, I've tried to make it work with other women, trust me. But it's never been right. Not like this. Not till you, Chloe."

"Bear, I don't—," I began.

"—let me finish, babe, please? When I met you that first time, I knew. I knew because something opened up in me, something about you ripped me wide open and crawled inside of me and never let go. It was like I'd been waiting for you my whole life. And then, when I saw you again, when we made love that first time —,"

"—that was not making love!" I protested.

"To me it was! To me, it was the beginning of everything that ever mattered. It was the confirmation that I was right all along. When I felt you around me, when I felt the perfection of our bodies fitting together like they were made from the same cloth, I knew, deep down, that you were the one."

"The one for what, though, Bear? What do you want with me? What is all of this even about?" I cried.

"That's a good question," he whispered, reaching into his coat and pulling out two small white boxes with shiny red ribbons. "I want to show you what my intentions are, Chloe. These are for you."

"What are they?" I asked. "The last time you gave me a present like this…"

"It's nothing like that. One is dependent on the other," he said, holding out one of the boxes to me. "Open this one first."

I sighed, shaking my head.

"Bear," I said. "I need to go."

"Just open them! Please! If you decide to leave afterwards, I'll kindly see you to the door of the plane myself."

"Fine," I said, my shaking hands taking the box from him. I pulled the end of the ribbon, untying the bow and letting it fall to the floor at my feet. Slowly, I opened the box and gasped when I saw the glittering diamond ring shining up at me.

"Bear!" I cried, my hand flying to my pounding heart. "Bear, this is too much—," I said, shaking my head.

He held the other box out to me, his eyes shining with love.

"Now open this one."

I opened the box quickly and pulled out a black velvet, diamond-studded choker.

"Chloe," he said, taking my hand, "I love you. I love you like the moon loves the stars. I'd be lost in this world without you by my side. I know this is confusing, I know it's all new and scary, but I promise you I'll take care of you for the rest of your life, I'll take you places you've never imagined. Yes, I have my issues, but I think our issues fit together perfectly. We're like opposite sides of the same coin, can't you see that? Being with you is like poetry, baby. We fit. Everything about us fits. Like the words strung together in a poem, as if they were made for each other. *You're* my poem, Chloe. You were meant for me, don't you see that? Opportunities like this, connections like ours, they only happen once in a lifetime, babe. We can't pass this up, we owe it to ourselves to give in to this love, to this life together. We'd be fools not to try."

I gasped, my head spinning, my heart racing as his eyes searched mine.

"But I need more from you, Chloe," he reached up, caressing my face. "You have to accept both sides of me, just as I have to accept both sides of you. I need you to be mine. I want you to wear my ring, but I want you to wear this, too," he said, brushing his fingers against the choker in my hand. "Do you understand, Chloe? I need you to be mine, in every way, forever and ever."

He sank to his knees, the ring between his fingers as he held it up to me.

"I love you. Please be my wife, Beauty," he pleaded.

I stared down at him, lost in his deep ocean eyes, lost in his enchanting words, lost in the simple fact that he'd told me he loved me.

My heart swelled with joy, with love, great waves of pleasure spilling out of my swollen heart. I couldn't think, all I could do was feel.

Maybe none of this made sense, but whatever it was, it was definitely love.

"Yes," I nodded slowly, tears falling down my face as he slipped the ring on my finger. He stood up, kissing me gently and then pulling away. He took the choker from my hands and placed it on my neck, fastening the buckle in the back, his fingers brushing against my skin and sending shivers down my spine.

"Look at you," he whispered, staring at me with eyes full of pride and love. "Who are you?"

A slow smile spread across my face, the velvet clinging tightly around my neck, the ring heavy on my hand, as my heart swelled with pride and pure happiness.

"I'm yours, Bear. I'm yours," I whispered through my tears.

His kiss was a thousand kisses, his love a thousand loves, and as we walked out of the airport arm in arm, I knew that our life together would be a thousand poems, worth a thousand heavens, in a thousand star-filled universes.

Chapter 30

Max drove us back to my apartment. We couldn't keep our hands or lips off of one another the entire drive and by the time we made it into the elevator, we were ready to rip each other's clothes off.

"I can't believe we're going to get married!" I said, laughing between kisses. "My mother is going to have a heart attack!"

"You let me deal with Matilda," he said, his tongue sliding along the skin of my neck. I shuddered against him, my body on fire with desire for him.

"Good luck with that," I muttered, my lips finding his again. He kissed me deeply, his tongue tangling with mine, searching for the magic we'd found together. The craziness of the entire situation was not lost on me, but at the moment, I didn't give a damn.

Everything Bear had said in the airport was true. Somehow, we fit together like two pieces of a puzzle and that was what I wanted to embrace.

I made a silent vow to reject the fear and doubts that had plagued me. I had plenty of help with the design job, I had plenty of time to do it and I was smart. As for the fear surrounding my relationship with Bear, well—I had Bear. That's all that mattered.

I made another vow to stay close to him, to communicate when I was feeling weird, to ask him questions if I needed to.

He loved me.

I'd never been so happy in my entire life.

Bear Dalton loved me and wanted to make me his wife. This beautiful, complex, masculine masterpiece of a human being wanted me by his side for the rest of his life.

I snaked my hands around his neck, pulling him closer while I kissed him, relishing the feel of his body against mine. The elevator dinged and we tumbled out into the hallway like a couple of horny teenagers.

He pushed me up against the wall of the hallway, his mouth searching mine, his hands running over my breasts as he pushed a thigh between my legs. I moaned against him, melting into the heat of his touch.

"Let's go inside," I said, pulling my mouth away and reaching down to grab a handful of his throbbing hardness. "I can't wait any longer!"

We turned together, our fingers laced together, the ring heavy and shiny on my finger.

We'd taken five steps when I saw him.

Standing at my doorway at the end of the hall, his face full of jealous anger and rage.

"Harlan!" I screamed in shock, my heart pounding so hard in my chest I thought it would burst. I felt Bear tense beside me.

"What are you doing here, Harlan?"

"Hello, Chloe," Harlan said, his voice seething. "I've come to take you back."

Before I could say a word, Bear stepped between us.

"Chloe's mine now," he growled. "You need to leave."

"I'm not going anywhere," Harlan scowled, reaching into his coat.

He pulled out a shiny, silver gun and pointed it straight at us.

To be continued in book 2 of the Taking Beauty Trilogy: CLAIMING BEAUTY.

Claiming Beauty is available now at Amazon in eBook and paperback!

Other books by Nikki Wild available in ebook or paperback at amazon.com:

Bad Boy Bikers:

ROUGHNECK (A Dark Biker Romance)

Saving Landon (A Bad Boy Biker Romance)

Saved by the Bad Boy (A Devil's Dragons Biker Romance)

Pride and Pregnancy (A Devil's Dragons Biker Romance)

Taming Grizz (A Devil's Dragons Biker Romance)

Rough Rider (Outlaw Kings Motorcycle Club)

British Bad Boys:

Royal Prick (A Bad Boy British Romance)

Arrogant Brit (A Bad Boy British Sports Romance)

Rock Hard (A Bad Boy British Rockstar

Romance)

Played (A Bad Boy British Romance)

Bad Boy Rockstars:

Illicit Behavior (A Bad Boy Rockstar Romance)

Rock Hard (A Bad Boy British Rockstar Romance)

Bad Boy Stepbrothers:

Lust (A Bad Boy Stepbrother Romance)

Richard (A Bad Boy Stepbrother Romance)

Bad Boy Billionaires:

Taking Beauty (Taking Beauty #1)

Claiming Beauty (Taking Beauty #2)

Owning Beauty (Taking Beauty #3 – available January 31st 2017)

45576086R00187

Made in the USA
San Bernardino, CA
11 February 2017